TAINTED TOWERS

EVORA JORDAN

First Edition

Edited by Beth Bruno, Ed.M, M.A.

EVORABOOKS, LLC
CANTON, CONNECTICUT

Copyright © 2005

ISBN: 0-9725071-4-0

Library of Congress Catalog Card Number: 0-9725071-4-0

Printed in the United States of America
by Tri-State Litho, Kingston, N.Y.

**Visit EvoraBooks on the World Wide Web at
www.BooksByEvora.com**

DEDICATION

To my family and friends who continue to
support and encourage my endeavors,
and
to the real Abby who lived and breathed
many of the events
that appear in this book!

ACKNOWLEDGMENTS

The author gratefully acknowledges the assistance of many people who have made it possible for me to investigate, write and publish *Tainted Towers*.

Connecticut Authors and Publishers Association Members:
Beth Bruno, Editor and President of CAPA
Dan Uitti, Technical Adviser, Webmaster and Vice President of CAPA
Jerry Labriola, M.D. Author of *Famous Crimes ReVisited*, Mentor, Past President and Historian of CAPA
Brian Jud, Book Marketing Works LLC., Avon, Ct. Mentor and Founder of CAPA

Deb Works, Westbrook, Maine, Researcher and Cohort
Sandor Bali, P.D., Owner/Pharmacy Manager, Arrow Pharmacy, Canton Village, Connecticut
Everett Newell, Miners Inc., Canton, Connecticut
Jay Kaplan, Director, Roaring Brook Nature Center, Canton, Connecticut
John Leahy, Host and Executive Producer of *Family Institutes*, a TV Series. Waterford, Connecticut
Cynthia Bercowetz, TV Host: *The Cynthia Bercowetz Show*, Bloomfield Access Television, Bloomfield, Connecticut

My family for their encouragement, love and faithful
support of my many ventures. They say: "Nothing
Mom does ever surprises us!"

Daughter, Diana Manner
Son-in-law, Ric
Grandsons, Karl and Kurt

Son, Barry Jordan
Daughter-in law, Christine
Granddaughter, Kelly and her husband, Jon
Grandson, Brian

EVORABOOKS LLC

DISCLAIMER

Although Tainted Towers is a work of fiction, it is inspired by true events. Many of the facts in this book were experienced by the author and some other parts are factual. The fiction in this book is purely a figment of the author's imagination.

Names of all characters and most of the place names are fiction. Any resemblance to persons living or dead is entirely coincidental.

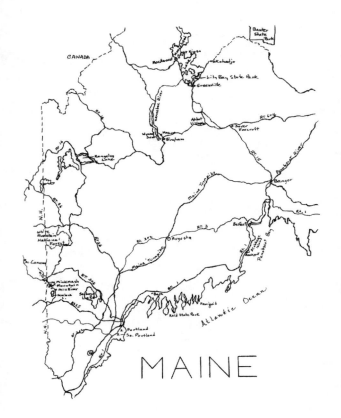

MAINE

Prologue

Marshwood Towers was doomed from its inception. This federal housing project was supposed to be built on the last available land on Hemlock Lake, land that had been designated wetland. To keep the locals and summer folks happy, Marshwood Towers would be a long, one-story U-shaped building that would not block anyone's view of Hemlock Lake. Twin, large towers would anchor each end of the building. The middle of the 'U' would be a screened pavilion with benches and a barbeque for all to enjoy. For their convenience, the recreation room and a laundry room were adjacent to this area.

Cement walkways would run along the front, lake side of the units, and go from the pavilion to the water. On the back side, a sidewalk would stretch up across the field to the shopping center. It would be just down the road apiece from the center of Mill River, an easy walking distance for the old folks and the disabled to access most of their needs.

For a few months every year the occupants would have beautiful clear, cool lake water for therapeutic exercise. The Mill River Mariner had offered free paddle boats for anyone who was able to peddle them. Mill River Bait and Tackle would build a wharf and supply free fishing equipment and bait for anyone who wanted to sit and fish. It sounded like paradise to all those who applied for one of the units.

The hopes and dreams were soon shattered. Marshwood Towers ended up being built half-way up the side of Mickmash Mountain on a granite ledge, two miles from the center of town!

A single lane, rutted dirt road wound up the mountain to Marshwood Towers. One mile up the road it made a sharp left turn and continued its way to the top. This federal housing project was built just past this curve and up the mountain to the right. The occupants had a beautiful view of the lake that they had planned on enjoying.

Half of the year the road was mud - mud so deep that many in the town swore that their cars totally disappeared during mud season and only reappeared when all the mud turned to dust. Every spring the dust would rise from the road like swarms of locusts, settling into the apartments like it was snowbird relatives back from wintering in Florida. No vehicles could travel this road for a few months every year. The handicapped couldn't get down the mountain, and nothing, not cars, fire trucks, ambulances nor the U.S. Postal trucks could get up.

Summer time was like a nightmare come true! The sun baked the dirt that had been moved in to level the land they lived on. The hot dirt penetrated everything: walkways, parking lots and their apartments. They couldn't escape the heat. There were no trees left to sit under, and their apartments had no air conditioning and no screens on the doors or windows.

The forecast for the tenants was predictable. These isolated humans became morbid, brooding, depressed and hostile people. Marshwood Towers was supposed to be their heaven on earth. It became their nether world. Every time they looked down at what was supposed to be their homes, they gazed at huge, imposing, two-story expensive condominiums that were rising from the ashes of the lakeside dreams of the destitute.

Over and over they would ask themselves, "What did we ever do to deserve this? How could something this hellish happen to us?"

Chapter One

Jason Cleeve sailed from Bristol, England in April 1630 aboard *The Swift*. His destination was Casco Bay on the coast of Maine. Jason settled in this region and three years later he founded Portland. His only son, Clayton, led many of the battles to save this area from hostile Indians who were backed by France. Portland was burned down and rebuilt a number of times before the war ended.

After the last Indian War, Capt. Clayton Cleeve was tired and weary. He bade farewell to his family, packed his belongings into his canoe and paddled down the Maine coast looking for solitude and peace. When he reached the mouth of the Saco River he was intrigued by the abundance of wildlife and fish. Leaving the Atlantic Ocean behind, he began the long, tedious journey up the river.

By the time Capt. Cleeve reached the source of the Saco, he knew he had found his home. There was a beautiful lake and majestic mountains rose high above a peaceful valley. Spring-fed mountain water had carved out a path down the mountain, cascading over cliffs into a river that fed into the lake. Tall, virgin forests surrounded this valley and Clay knew this was where he was supposed to be.

There were Indians living in this valley, a region they called Mickmash Land. These Indians were far removed from the French, English and Indian conflicts and they greeted Capt. Cleeve with kindness and curiosity. Clay was an imposing figure, tall, handsome and outgoing. He quickly made friends with the Chief by sharing the goods from his canoe. The Chief repaid him by giving Clay his oldest daughter.

Nine months later Clayton Cleeve, Jr. was born and the Cleeve dynasty began. Clay fathered four sons and became the new 'chief' of the area. He built a mill on the river, the first of many enterprises, and renamed it Mill River. Eventually the entire valley area became part of the town of Mill River. Clay was a benevolent leader, treating everyone, including the dwindling Indian population, with kindness and respect.

Mill River is still a Cleeve dominated area that reeks of the Cleeve's influence. There is a Cleeve Lumber Yard, Cleeve Manufacturing, Cleeve Pharmacy, Cleeve High School, Cleeve Construction Company and a Cleeve Ball Field. Almost everyone in the town claims a connection to old Capt. Cleeve.

There are no full-blooded Indians left in Mill Town. Years ago the few remaining tribal members packed their sparse belongings and joined up with others on a reservation in Nova Scotia. They left behind a legacy but there is nobody left who would dare to mention that all the Cleeves have Indian blood flowing through their veins.

Also gone is the kindness and graciousness of old Capt. Cleeve. Clayton Cleeve IV is arrogant, bigoted and pompous, the King who reigns over His territory.

Clayton IV's younger brother, Clarence, has all of the same despicable traits but lacks the backbone of his older brother. He brags that the

only things he can do better than his big brother
are drink more liquor and bed more women!

Chapter Two

Clayton Cleeve IV was not the first Cleeve to use his power and prestige to control the Town of Mill River, but he was by far the most mercenary. Under his regime the back side and summit of Mickmash Mountain were cleared of all the trees that were then turned into lumber in his Lumber Mill. Once the trees were all destroyed, he moved in his rock crushing equipment. The Cleeve Construction Company would have a source of gravel for years.

The families that lived on the far side of the mountain were more than just a little upset by the constant pounding from the quarry. The noise and additional truck and heavy equipment traffic permeated the whole neighborhood. Added to their frustration was the knowledge that there was absolutely nothing they could do about it. Most of these families were young couples struggling to make a living on the meager wages they were paid for the work they did for one of the Cleeve Companies. There was a sign prominently displayed in all of the plants: "Don't Ever Bite The Hand That Feeds You!" They all knew what this message meant: "Keep your mouth shut or get fired!"

Once things calmed down about his mountain top enterprise, Clay cleared an area on the north side of the mountain. He had the area leveled off and a ditch dug around the outer periphery. The course of the spring water that rushed down the mountain and through the lakeside wetlands was diverted into his 'moat'. There would never again be a wetland classification for that area.

Then Clay built a drawbridge over the moat and built his fortress. The long, winding, muddy road led up to his citadel. He would replace this with a two-lane tarred royal road someday but for now Clay had no desire to make it easy for the infidels to visit. Clay spent many contented hours sitting in his castle looking out over his domain, basking in the knowledge that the heart of his kingdom was secure.

Chapter Three

Clay began having strategy meetings at his Fortress. Nobody was ever invited to attend these meetings except his brother. Clay kept no minutes of these meetings and when the Cleeve Board of Directors met, they heard only what Clay wanted them to hear.

Today's meeting was no exception. Clay got a fresh cup of coffee and mixed Clarence a martini. They went out to the veranda where they could look out over their land.

"We won again; I knew we would!"

Clarence raised his glass, gulped down much of the liquor and said, "OK, tell me how you pulled this one off."

"No problem at all. The best move I made was to get Molly elected as the Code Enforcement Officer and then buy her off. Money sure as hell worked in this case."

Slurring his words Clarence laughingly said, "What a horny bitch she is."

"You can say that again! She would shack up with anybody or anything!"

"I still don't know how you got that arrogant Wetland Commissioner on our side of the fence!"

Clay began laughing. "Oh, I just showed him a photograph that I happened to have. After he saw the photo of him and Molly totally naked going at it on the top of his desk, the rest was easy."

"Good strategy, Clay, fix me another drink and tell me what's next on the agenda."

"Well, the best is yet to come. We have the HUD contract under our thumbs now. Money talked again! We're moving the Federal Housing project up onto the west side of our mountain, and we'll begin building the high rise condos on the former wetland property."

"My God, you're good at this."

"We'll get started on both places at the same time but go slower on the Condos. Once we begin we can control the price better. The rich snowbirds will be begging to buy them. We'll use up all the leftover supplies that we have in the warehouse for the Federal Housing job and cut corners everywhere we can. We sure as hell know the Code Enforcement Officer isn't going to give us any grief! As long as we keep Molly on the take and keep her in spending money, we're in control of her. We'll more than make back what we paid her by cutting costs on the Federal Units."

"Won't we get in trouble with HUD if we cut corners?"

"Don't be so damn dumb! I've paid them off and they sure as hell won't give a shit what we do!"

Clarence helped himself to another drink and raised his glass. "You done good Clay, I salute you." He gulped down the martini, stared blurry-eyed out over their kingdom and passed out.

Clay looked down at him in disgust. "I'm in command of this kingdom. Who in hell cares what you think, you poor excuse for a Cleeve."

Chapter Four

I'm Hannah Gray and I am one of the many descendants of Capt. Cleeve. I don't brag about this connection but I don't curtsy and salute when I pass Clayton on the street. Neither do I go the other way if I see him coming. But it seems like Clayton and Clarence both go out of their way to avoid me.

The Cleeve Construction Company was one of the two companies that had to pay me $52,000 for construction fraud on a house they built for me on the mountain. Not only did I win the case, I did it without a lawyer! To add to their displeasure, I wrote about this fraud in one of my books, *Tainted Sand*. Clay and Clarence were livid because nobody had ever opposed them. It was even rumored around town that I should watch my back, a rumor no doubt started and perpetuated by the two of them!"

This didn't create a problem for me that I hadn't already lived with. I'm a retired everything. I've been a teacher, counselor, politician, farmer, carpenter, office manager, logging truck driver and held a number of other jobs I'd rather not mention. You name it, and I've probably done it, and loved every minute of it. Well, almost every minute. Sometimes I tend to exaggerate. I have worked on many child abuse and rape cases, however, where my life was threatened. Before I helped establish the 3rd Rape Counsel in Maine, our group got Crisis Intervention Training, a form of self-defense training. I had the chance to train many others. I could, if I ever had to, kill a person with my bare hands! Living on the edge isn't so terrifying if you know how to protect yourself.

I'm retired now and working at changing the definition of retirement. Although I still counsel abuse victims, I'm spending most of my time writing books, then publishing and peddling them. I'm also doing my own research and investigations. It's a fascinating way to learn new things and see a lot of the world. Of

15

course, sometimes I get into deep water, which serves to keep my brain in gear, helping me to stay resourceful, competent and happy. Life is good. However, you can bet that I not only know how but that I do watch my back – a lot of the time!

I have no intention of changing the way I live because of two egotistical, self-proclaimed members of Mill River royalty. At the same time, while I was still living down the road apiece and on the same mountain as Clay, I took extra precautions. I kept my part German Shepherd, part Norwegian Elkhound, Annie Love, close by and on a leash when she was outside. I locked my doors day and night. I kept my cell phone on me and I notified all of my friends in the surrounding area police departments that my life had been threatened and that I was selling the mountain home and moving back to the lake.

Even though I was well trained and worked on many difficult cases, it was a relief to move out of town. I could swim every day, peddle my paddle boat along the shoreline, and walk the back roads. From my favorite place to sleep on the front porch, I could listen to the loons crying most of the night and watch the Piliated Woodpeckers while I ate my breakfast. I tried to think of the move as a perfect opportunity rather than running away from two depraved brothers.

Chapter Five

It didn't take me long to settle back into my early morning lakeside routine. I always wake up before the sun, a habit that began years ago growing up on the farm. The first one in the morning to get to the barn got a choice of milking the cows or cleaning out the trough behind them. I never missed a morning milking the cows! We didn't have milking machines back then and my hands still ache whenever I think about this.

I made a cup of really hot, black coffee, threw on a terrycloth robe and meandered slowly towards the lake. I can think of no better way to start my day than being the only human on the lake who isn't sleeping. Ayah, there may be others up but if I can't hear them from here, they don't count. There is an abundance of early birds, however, and this means as much to me as the lack of humans. Chickadees, mourning doves, blue jays, sparrows and my pileated woodpeckers are part of my early morning enjoyment.

I put my cup of coffee on the dock, discarded my robe and slowly swam the beautiful, sandy cove and back. I always try to follow this routine from Mother's Day in May to my birthday in November. It isn't always possible to keep to this schedule; it depends on how soon the ice forms in the fall and how soon it disappears in the spring.

This morning was a little chilly and I quickly wrapped my robe around me, grabbed my coffee from the deck and hurried back to the front porch. I tried to settle into my favorite chair but I was restless. I knew I should be adding pages to the next book but I couldn't seem to get past worrying a little bit about Sam. I hadn't heard from him for quite a long time and I missed hearing his voice.

Chapter Six

Sam is a retired Maine State Police Detective and an excellent investigator. Although small in stature – five foot, seven inches tall and 180 pounds soaking wet – be still my heart – his intelligence and graciousness toward everyone far overshadow his physical being. I've worked with Sam on many tough cases and have never seen him lose his cool, calm demeanor. Nor has he ever been rude or insulting to anyone. He is the epitome of professionalism.

Sam is also handsome and has a beautifully proportioned face. His brown sparkling eyes, straight nose and mouth go together just right. And, if that isn't enough, he wears clothes that make him look quite dapper.

Sam and I met years ago when we were both working on the same rape case. Our rapport was immediately apparent. He began learning about the emotional and physical devastation an abused person has suffered, and I gained an immense amount of knowledge about the investigation process. We have worked many cases since and our admiration and respect for each other has remained and grown over the years.

For many years our relationship was strictly professional, but after both of our spouses developed terminal illnesses and passed away within a year of each other, Sam and I reached out to each other for emotional support.

We are now very comfortable with our independent lifestyles. Sam is away a lot of the time, working undercover for a federal agency. We both enjoy the intensity of our jobs, many times living just below sea level. We think of our time together as our hobby, something we do in our spare time for fun and relaxation.

Chapter Seven

I finished my coffee, made a second cup and talked myself into settling down to work. When all else fails, I can always crank up the computer and do some research. Computer work is my least favorite part of being an author and self-publisher. It works, however, in getting me back on track. Today was no exception and I was able to forget worrying about Sam as I reviewed and printed information about HUD's problems relating to construction fraud. My friend, Abby, would love reading this stuff.

Although I had moved back to my home on Hemlock Lake, I spend as much time as possible trying to help Abby. She loves to swim and I often drive over to her apartment in the housing project to bring her to the lake. I try to time my visits so that we can eat out at one of the many excellent restaurants in Mill River.

She always has a new story to tell about how mismanaged the Housing was. Nobody seemed to care that it was not built to specifications and that local regulations were totally ignored.

There were two long buildings erected along the side of the mountain. Each one had ten apartments – five back to back. Regulations required one vent stack for each bathroom, but these buildings had two stack for ten bathrooms. There were supposed to be vents for kitchen and bathroom, but these buildings had one for every two apartments.

One of Abby's biggest complaints was the odors that whiffed into her apartment from the apartment that backed up to hers. The man who lived there worked part-time at the local dump, and he was always bringing home 'things' he picked up on his job. He would cook these 'dead animals' that had been discarded and the horrendous smell spread throughout Abby's place. One time she tried putting tinfoil in the vent between the apartments, but was forced into removing it. One of the inspectors told her, "That's against regulations, you know that Abby, so take it out of the vent!"

I listened to her horror stories and shared her frustration at the fraudulent disregard for the rules by the same authorities that forced the tenants to follow the rules! And, as might be expected, I became more and more involved in Marshwood Towers and vowed to do whatever it would take to 'fix' this horrible situation.

This investigation evolved into a frightening, complicated, life threatening scheme of graft, corruption and murder. I knew that I would have to include all of this in my next murder/mystery novel. I had excellent feedback on the word 'tainted' from the readers of *"Tainted Sand."* This new book would be titled *"Tainted Towers."*

Chapter Eight

Abby, my friend and confidant, is one of the occupants at Marshwood Towers. She is the only young, physically handicapped occupant of this 'hell hole,' as she calls it. Her pat answer each time someone asks her about the problems living in this place is, "Well, so what else is new? Money talks you say? Sure it does! Graft, bribery and fraud are everyday occurrences. So what if we're surrounded by deceitful, dishonest swindlers. Shit happens! Get a life!" But Abby refuses to take any of this lying down!

Abby may be physically handicapped, but she is mentally superior. She is young enough to be my daughter and wise enough to be my grandmother. Her wacky sense of humor is matched only by her uncanny ability to do anything, especially if it hints at being illicit.

Abby is a large lady, six feet tall, hefty and strong as a bullock. She tends to dress either in cut-off stretch pants and oversized sneakers, (with no socks ever), or flamboyantly in bright long skirts and t-tops. She keeps things – keys, money, bones for all the neighbors' dogs, lock picks, and only she knows what else – hidden deep between her ample breasts. She has long, straight brown hair and sometimes wears it pulled back into a twist or high on her head. Her hair styles, combined with a face that has no distinctive flaws, make it difficult for people to remember what she looks like – a definite advantage when she is up to her tricks.

Abby has a passion for all things outdoors. Bird feeders, flowers, cats and dogs were the only pleasant allowances the Federal Housing Authority made. Abby took advantage of these 'exceptions' to the strict rules and her flower garden was spectacular. She would lower herself out of her wheelchair to the ground and with her strong upper body would lift herself around the garden plot. She spent hours planting and weeding, not just in front of her apartment but in all the others, too.

Most of the time that Abby spent outdoors, she was watched over by a Bald Eagle that had a nest high in an old tree behind the buildings. She would 'talk' to the eagle, mimicking the cackling sound – kik – ik – ik – ik, kleek - kleek –kleek so accurately that the eagle would answer her. When the eagle left her nest she would make a wide sweep around the buildings, swooping low over Abby. She told me that this gave her the chance to imagine soaring with the eagle!

Abby also watched over all the other tenants. They were all senior citizens and she had a natural talent for making them feel like wonderful human beings. There were many times when her former work as a nurses aide at the local hospital came in handy here. However, she was the only younger, handicapped person living there, and there were also many times that she felt discouraged and helpless!

This morning Abby was sitting by her picture window enjoying a second cup of coffee and watching the birds vying for the seeds in the birdfeeder. She loved being able to see them up so close. Her favorite birds were the

Chickadees. Their black cap and bib and snowy white cheeks were a delightful contrast to the Red Cardinals and Blue Jays. They would scurry around on the feeder, scratching and pecking at seeds and each other while others whistled their chick-a-dee-dee-dee song as they waited in the bushes for their turn. Abby felt that the Chickadees were like her, dull outsiders amongst color, yet busy all the time.

Chapter Nine

Twelve years ago Abby had been in an automobile accident that left her unable to walk. In a flash she went from being a productive hospital employee to a member of the State's impoverished group. She now needed yet another hip replacement but first she had to lose a lot of weight. She knew that the longer she stayed in the Housing, the harder everything was going to be to get back on her own. But she hadn't yet been able to find the strength to deal with dieting. She wasn't physically able to exercise nor was she mentally ready to give up food.

Abby was the youngest tenant in the Housing and she tried to compensate for her handicap by helping all the older people whenever she could. She was always checking to make sure they were taking their medicine.

She baked cookies and took some with her when she visited them. She helped them do housework, get dressed, do their laundry and washed their dishes. She would listen to their sad stories and try to encourage them to take better care of themselves.

Susan, in Unit 10, was her biggest frustration. Abby was trying to get Susan to report her son, Pete, to the police. He had been stealing her pain medicine for over a year! Abby figured that Pete had been substituting her OC with an over-the-counter pain medicine. Susan would tolerate the pain for a few weeks and then would call the Rescue Unit, and be taken to the Fall River Hospital. The hospital doctors would give her a new prescription for the OC and Pete would give her a ride home.

One time Abby had followed the Rescue Unit to the hospital. She hid out there and watched Pete come and leave with Susan. They stopped at the Mill Town Pharmacy and then returned to his mother's apartment. It seemed incomprehensible that no one ever questioned how often she arrived in the Emergency Room!

After months of discussing this with her, Abby had finally convinced Susan to tell Pete that she was calling the cops if he stole the pills again.

Chapter Ten

"What in hell are you doing here, Pete? I guess you didn't believe me when I said I'd call the cops the next time you stole my pain medicine. I'm calling them right now."

She reached for the telephone and started to dial 911.

Pete yanked the phone away from her. "You'll call over my dead body, Ma, and stop yelling! Calm down before you have another heart attack! I believed you and I'm off the OC for good. I just stopped in to thank you for forcing me to go cold turkey, 'cause there ain't no way I'm going to spend any time in jail."

"I've heard that over and over, Pete. How many more times do you think I can get away with lying for you? You take my OxyContin® pills and substitute Entrie Coated Aspirin and they sure don't help much. I stand the pain as long as I can, then call 911. The Rescue Unit takes me to the Fall River Hospital. They give me a new prescription; you get it filled and steal the pills. I have had enough of this. I can't take it anymore – Oh, my heart – get me some of my digoxin pills – hurry!"

"Sure, Ma, here let me help you sit up. There, that's better, open up and I'll put them in your mouth. Great, Ma, now drink some water. I'll put these pillows behind your back. OK, feeling better? You have to believe me; I ain't addicted to OC anymore."

"That's the best news I've heard in a long time, Pete. I'm so proud of you. You'll never know how much I've worried about you!"

"Well, you should be proud of me, and you'll never have to worry about me again." He took his mother's hand and said, "Ma, there's something I need to ask you, like how did you find out I had switched the OC pills with Entrie Coated Aspirin? You say you can't see much at all so how did you know the pills weren't OxyContin®?"

"I didn't notice Pete, but one day when Abby was here checking up on me, I needed some medicine. She went into the bathroom to get the pills and noticed that they didn't look quite right. She was really upset!"

"How in hell could she tell the difference?"

"She wasn't absolutely sure, so she took one of my pills up to Miss Wood. She is taking OC pills too. She compared her pills with mine and they didn't match. Since you're the only other person who visits me, it was pretty easy to figure out that you were the one stealing them."

"That figures, she's such a noisy bitch, I should pound the shit out of her!"

"You'll do no such thing, Pete; Abby is the only one in the Housing that helps us. She's a kind, smart, decent person and she cares about all of us."

"Ayah, she's a dandy alright. Is this Miss Wood the same stupid old maid 5th grade teacher that I had?"

"She's not stupid, Peter; you shouldn't talk about her like that. After your father passed away, she tried really hard to help you learn to cope without him!"

"Sure as hell didn't help me much! That's enough of this kind of talk. I brought you some special tea; it's supposed to be really good for

34

the heart. You sit here quietly while I warm it up for you."

On the way to the kitchen Pete stopped in the bathroom, downed some of his mothers OC and gulped down a glass of water. He was really upset to think that Abby knew what he had been doing. He stood for a minute, trying to calm down. "What in hell am I going to do now? I'll fix that bitch if it's the last thing I ever do! Dear Abby is going to pay dearly for butting her fat face into my business!" He got his flask from his coat pocket, poured the contents into his Ma's favorite mug and zapped it in the microwave. He sang a little tune while he waited for the special brew to heat: Got along without you before I met you, going to get along without you now. Going to find me someone just as sick, cause I never liked you anyhow!" He laughed at how clever he was to have found out about Abby and a new source of OC.

This was turning out to be much easier than he figured it would be. Dear old Mom gets extra dioxin pills and then a mug of nice, warm, full-of-digitalis, foxglove tea. He got the mug of tea from the microwave. Fighting back the urge to laugh, he stood in the kitchen until he regained his composure. "You old bitch, this is going to be service you would die for!"

"I added lots of sugar to this tea 'cause it doesn't taste too good, Ma, but the Doc said it would help you a lot. He said that you will feel a whole lot better after you take this – so drink it down, like a good girl."

"You're right, Pete, this smells and tastes horrid, I don't if I can tolerate drinking this!"

"Sure you can Mom. You must remember how you always told me that the worse it tasted, the better it was for you and that I could have a cookie when I drank it all? Well, Ma, take your own advice and drink it. It's really going to make you feel better. And, I'll get you a cookie if you drink it all real fast."

"Ayah, I did always say that, didn't I." She smiled at her son and gulped down the bitter-tasting liquid.

"Good, Ma, now let me take these pillows out from behind you so you can lie down. I'll leave so you can get some sleep, and you don't have to remind me, I'll leave the door unlocked when I leave. Thanks, again Mom for forcing me to do this, but I just don't understand how you could put your only child in jail."

"I could because I love you, Pete. When I found out that you had been stealing my OC I felt so bad I just wanted to die! I knew that I had to find the strength to do whatever I needed to do to help you! I couldn't keep quite and enable you to be a drug addict any longer!"

As he left the bedroom he muttered, "Yah, love you too – you bitch. Sleep tight." He stopped only to snatch the bottle of OxyContin® from the bathroom, locked the outside door and left for the last time.

Chapter Eleven

She slept for awhile but woke up screaming with terrible stomach cramps. Her head was throbbing. Her bed and everything in the room looked fuzzy. Then she set up as the bed, and the telephone began floating around the room, and they all turned into a brilliant blue color. She lay back down trying to figure out what was happening to her. She began floating all around the room! "I don't believe this is happening to me, what ever is the matter? I have never had anything like this happen before!" She started holding tightly to the headboard so she wouldn't float away. "Oh, my God, this isn't working! Now the bed is floating around too!" She put her arms over her head trying to cradle it to keep it from hitting the ceiling.

"I'm going to be sick, how can I possibly get from here to the bathroom, everything is floating around. I don't dare let go of the bed; I'll float away if I do. I'll never be able to catch the toilet or the sink!"

"Oh, my God, Pete must have put digitalis in the tea!" She knew she was dying and tears streamed down her face as she realized that her son was so addictive to OC that he would rather kill her than try to break his habit.

Terrible thoughts raced through her brain, pain slammed into her body, she screamed in agony and then began laughing hysterically. "I'm going insane, poisoned with foxglove, just like Van Gogh, everything blurry and spiraling around and around! He must have felt just like I'm feeling when he added the foxglove plant on the table when he painted his physician, Dr. Gachet. Oh, dear God, how can I think of Van Gogh when I hurt so much? I'm really losing my mind! Somehow I must get to the telephone and call for help."

Sharp pains jabbed at her chest and her whole intestinal tract was on fire. Sheets of dizziness tore through her whole body! She was sweating so much that everything was totally wet. She was so tired that she didn't think she could move.

Somehow she got the strength to let go of the headboard. She made a desperate lunge across the bed and managed to capture the telephone!

She dialed 911 – for the last time.

Chapter Twelve

Abby was just finishing her coffee when something scared the birds and they scattered in all directions. She looked down the hill and saw Pete running to his car in the parking lot. Great, that poor excuse for a son had visited his deal old Mom again. No doubt the Rescue Unit would be there in a few days to transport her to the hospital again.

It was this kind of behavior that made Abby both mad and sad. Nobody seemed to care enough to even wonder why Susan kept going to the hospital. Wasn't there anybody at the hospital who kept track of how many times a patient showed up there? How many other patients did they enable to get drugs more often than they should? Each time Susan returned with a new prescription for OxyContin® and each time Pete took the prescription and got it filled. Then he substituted it with Entrie Coated Aspirin! And nobody seemed to give a damn about what was happening.

Pete hadn't been around since he got the last prescription filled two days before. He had left the OC with his mother. Abby had hoped that he wouldn't ever come here again. Exasperated by her inability to help Susan, she groaned, "What a shame, he is so addicted that he wasn't even afraid of his mother calling the cops."

Abby forced herself to gather up the clothes to take to the laundry. She piled them into a basket and put the basket on her lap and headed across the path to the road. She had to go all the way around the road to the far side of the lower units to get to the laundry room, the mail room and the parking lot. There were only steep stairs connecting the upper and lower units. She had just reached the laundry room when she heard sirens coming up the hill. There was no doubt in her mind – she knew exactly who they were coming to get. She set the laundry basket onto the floor and hurried back to Susan's apartment.

Two EMT's were banging on the door and yelling. "How in hell are we supposed to help someone if we can't get into the house? Why would someone call us and not unlock the door?"

Abby wheeled up behind them and said, "If you guys will move out of the way and let me get by you, I'll unlock the door for you."

"Well, for God's sake hurry, and then get out of our way!"

Abby turned her back to them and wheeled close to the door. She reached between her ample bosoms, and pulled out her lock picks. It only took her a few minutes to pick the lock. She moved her wheelchair out of the way and sat waiting to see what had happened. She fought to overcome her apprehension that something terrible had happened to Susan. She knew that her friend never locked her door, which meant that Pete locked it when he left! Why would he lock his mother inside?

Her thoughts were interrupted when one of the EMT's came running out of the unit. He raced across the grass and got a stretcher from the ambulance and rushed back inside.

As he ran by her, Abby said, "You can't get her out the door on a stretcher!"

He yelled back, "Lady, just stay out of our way and keep quiet. If we want your help we'll ask for it."

Inside the house, both men were sweating as they hurried to get Susan ready to transport to the hospital. Her pulse was erratic and her blood pressure was very high. Her body was convulsing and she was moaning constantly. It was obvious from her soiled clothing and the foul smell that she had vomited and had diarrhea. They looked at each other and one mouthed, "Overdosed!"

They quickly turned her onto her side and made sure her mouth was free of vomit. One ran into the bathroom and grabbed a large towel from the rack. They wrapped it around Susan like a diaper. Then they pulled the top sheet off the bed and wrapped that around her. They laid her on her side onto the stretcher, and strapped her down. They picked up the stretcher and hurried toward the bedroom door.

They stopped at the doorway. That's as far as they were able to go. The hallway was too narrow to make a turn into the hall. One of them yelled, "For God's sake, who in hell would build homes for the elderly and handicapped and not make them assessable for emergencies?"

By this time Abby had wheeled herself into the house and maneuvered her wheelchair down the narrow hall. "You're absolutely right, and even if you could get out into the hall, you couldn't get the stretcher out through the entryway!"

"How in hell are we supposed to get her out of here?"

"You have to turn the screws on the inside of the bedroom window and take the window out to get her out of here. That was the contractor's solution after we complained to them that we couldn't get a stretcher down the hall, nor out around the entryway from the living room to the outside. It sure isn't a very good solution but it works."

They put the stretcher back on the bed. One of them crawled across the bed and using the wall to balance himself, turned the screws and pulled the window into the bedroom. Then he picked up one end of the stretcher and pulled it closer to the open window. He backed out the window, stepped down onto the ground and reached for his end of the stretcher. His partner crawled onto the bed and took the other end.

"Damn, it's too wide to fit out the window. What in hell do we do now?"

Abby quietly said, "You have to tip one side of it up and take it out kitty-corner."

"Hell, lady, that won't work either!"

"Yes, it will, I've been taken out that way before, so don't argue with me anymore, just do it and get Susan to the hospital before it's too late!"

The man outside reached in and between them they got the stretcher tipped up sideways. They held Susan's head in place with one hand as they forced the stretcher through the opening. The man on the back end had to crawl across the bed and then lean out the window to set the stretcher on the ground. He leaped out the window and they hurried their patient into the ambulance.

While this was going on, Abby had gone back outside. She watched as they ran by her – Susan looked terrible. Abby knew that she wouldn't be coming home again. She whispered, "God be with you, Susan."

"I'll stay here until someone can put the window back in," she shouted.

Nobody heard her.

Chapter Thirteen

The sharp ring of the telephone put a stop to my research. I rushed to answer it, hoping that it would be Sam calling. It was Abby, and she was crying. "Could you come over Hannah? I'm in Susan's apartment and I think that Pete must have poisoned her. I think she has been killed!"

"I'll be right there, don't touch or move anything. Are you alright? Have you called the cops?"

"No, I don't know for sure if she's gone, but she looked dead when the EMT's left with her. They had a terrible time getting her out of here; it took them a long time and I'm really afraid Pete did kill her!"

I grabbed my purse, camera and cell phone and headed for the mountain. Hopefully there would be enough evidence to put Pete away for a very long time. It was hard to imagine how he could have been stealing her meds for so long without getting caught. What a poor excuse for a human.

I took all the back roads ignoring any speed limits and soon pulled into the parking lot. Grabbing my things, I quickly walked up to Susan's place. Abby was sitting outside the door, tears streaming down her face. I bent down and hugged her, crying with her.

"I shouldn't have talked her into telling him she was going to tell the cops.! She'd be alive now if I'd kept out of it.! I should have known better than to try to help her.! What a fool I've been to think I could help her.!"

"You did the right thing, Abby. He was and is a drug addict. He would have killed her sometime whether you intervened or not. You did what you had to do to try to help her. Nobody else cared enough to intervene. Now let's go inside and do a little snooping."

Abby wheeled slowly into the living room. I followed her. The air was foul but I closed the outside door behind me. We had a lot to do before we called the hospital to check on her condition. Until then, we didn't need any of the neighbors coming around to see what was happening.

"We have to be careful not to touch or move anything. You've been here a lot, Abby; sit in one spot and look around to see if anything is missing or in the wrong place. I'll take a picture before we look around and another when we move on." I got a pad and pen from my purse and started taking notes to go with the pictures.

"Everything looks normal here."

I took some pictures and made some notes.

"OK, lets try the kitchen next."

"There's a tea bag on the counter and the microwave door is open. Susan wouldn't have left them like that!"

"Alright, you're doing really good, Abby."

I took a picture of the counter with these items on it and made more notes.

"Let's try the bathroom next."

"The cops were everywhere here and in the bedroom. They could have moved everything."

"They sure could have but just sit, look and think, Abby. Picture the area in your mind. What is or isn't where it should be? Concentrate really hard and try hard to see beyond the mess!"

She sat quietly a short time. The silence was ominous. Somewhere in the apartment a clock was ticking and the sound seemed to crowd out everything else. It seemed like a long time before Abby spoke."

"The pill bottle that was supposed to have the OC in it is missing. Susan always kept it where she could easily reach it, just to the left of the sink."

"Good going, Abby!"

I continued my picture taking and note routine.

"Now let's finish up in the bedroom."

"The bedroom is a total shambles. I was right here with the cops. They had a terrible time getting her out of here and they tore the bedding apart to cover her up. They also took a towel from the bathroom to use as a diaper." Tears began streaming down Abby's face.

I gave her a hug. "You're doing just great!"

51

"I hope so, but I'm so terribly angry!"

"Try to settle down, Abby; try to look beyond the mess. If there is anyway to nail Pete with murdering his mother, I need your help."

"Her favorite mug is on the bedside table, Hannah; she never brought it in here."

"All right! Good for you! You've done a great job, Abby. "Let me get more pictures, and then let's get out of here!"

"The window is still right where the EMT's left it. I can't leave until the window gets put back in!"

"Well, considering how many times in the past we've moved, fixed, lifted and cut down things, let's get to it!"

I took one more picture and put things back into my purse and put it into the pocket on the wheelchair.

With Abby on the outside and me on the inside, standing on the bed leaning out, we lifted the window up and got it partially onto the sill. Abby moved one corner a little more and the window slid into place. I turned the bolts locking the window and crawled back across the bed.

Even though I wanted to just leave and get away from the dreadful smell, I went to the kitchen instead, found a plastic bag and went back to the bathroom and got some toilet paper. The odor was beginning to get to me as I hurried to the bedroom. I very carefully wrapped up Susan's favorite mug and put it into the bag. Another quick look around and I left, leaving the dreadful smell of death behind me.

We headed for Abby's apartment. It seemed strange to have so much going on yet none of the other residents were out and about. When I mentioned this to Abby she just shrugged her shoulders and said, "No one gives a damn about anybody else here; they're all too busy trying to keep themselves alive!"

"Why don't you come home with me for awhile, Abby, and get away from all of this? We can go swimming and sit around watching nothing, just relaxing. You can stay all night or I'll bring you back here whenever you want."

"Thanks, Hannah, but I'm really OK and I want to be here when the cops come, if they ever do! I'm just so thankful that you were here for me. You are a wonderful friend. I'll call you later."

We hugged and I headed for the lake.

Chapter Fourteen

I was concerned about Abby and called her early the next morning.

"I was just going to call you, Hannah. Can you come over today? I'm worried about something."

"Sure can, Abby. I'll stop at McDonald's and bring breakfast, OK?"

"That sounds good. I'll make coffee. See you soon."

We settled down in her living room. The big plate glass window was surrounded by flourishing house plants. Outside the birds were busy flitting back and forth from her garden to the bird houses that Abby had built. We sat and silently ate our breakfast, enjoying the birds and the coolness of the morning.

Later in the day the sun would shine directly into this room and even with the drapes

55

closed the area would be stifling hot! There was no ventilation in these apartments, no air conditioners, no windows you could open, hence no screens. The only way to get fresh air was to leave the front door, the only door, open and there was no screen door.

As Abby refilled our coffee cups, tears began falling down her face. She wiped them off and took a deep breath.

"Hannah, I'm real worried about Miss Wood. I told Susan that I had compared her OC to Miss Wood's to prove to her that Pete was stealing her medicine. I think she may have told this to Pete. If she did, just as soon as he runs out of his mothers OC, he's apt to start stealing from Miss Wood."

"If Susan did tell Pete, then you probably are right to worry about Miss Wood. But he may not know how you found out that he was switching pills."

"I was sitting here in the dark late last night and someone was outside the upper units. Whoever it was had on dark clothes and was creeping along very slowly. I wouldn't have noticed except I saw a moving shadow so I watched more closely. Whoever it was continued to Miss Wood's place, stopped a few minutes, then continued past the empty end unit and disappeared."

"Could it have been someone who lives here?"

"No, I waited a minute and then I slowly opened my door and I heard a car leave the lower parking lot. I'm really worried, Hannah!"

"Sounds like you have a good reason to worry."

"I was awake all night trying to think of some way to keep Miss Wood safe from Pete. I think I'm going to stay in the vacant unit next to her so if he bothers her I can catch him!"

"He knows you too well, Abby. He'd spot you in a minute and would probably enjoy getting back at you."

"But I feel so terrible to have caused so many problems, Hannah, I have to do something!"

We sat in silence for awhile, both trying to come up with a workable plan to protect Miss Wood and catch Pete in the process.

"One thing I can do, Abby, is to meet with the Hospital Director and try to find out what needs fixing on their end."

"Great idea. I've been concentrating so much on Pete's role in this that I've overlooked theirs."

I'll meet with him alone first. Then if he needs more info, will you meet with him?"

"You know I will, but I agree that you should meet alone with him first. We don't want to come on too strong."

Our thoughts were interrupted when a truck came up the hill, drove across the lawn and backed up to Susan's apartment. Pete and another man began loading everything from the unit into the truck.

Abby wheeled over to the door, opened it and sat watching them. When the last item was loaded, Pete started to get into the truck. He turned and looked down at Abby. He cocked his finger, pointed it gun fashion at her and yelled, "Bang, bang, you're dead meat, Fatso!"

"Well, Abby, I guess that takes care of your plan. There's no way you can try to protect Miss Wood and remain safe yourself!"

Abby silently nodded her agreement.

"The police haven't been here yet?"

"No they haven't and I've been here all of the time."

We really need to let the police know what's going on, Abby. They probably won't do anything, but we need this on the record. I'll start by contacting one of my State Police friends and see if we can come up with a plan. Meanwhile, pack a bag. You're coming home with me for awhile."

"That's running away. I don't want to run away from this."

"I know you don't but it's going to take both of us and then some to catch Pete. You won't be any good to us dead!"

"I'll stay inside, out of sight, but I have to be able to keep a watch on Miss Wood."

We sat quietly for a few minutes.

"I need to do this, Hannah. Meet with the police as soon as you can. I'll go along with any plan you all come up with, but I have to be right here 'til then."

I knew that I wasn't going to convince her to leave. We hugged and I returned to the lake via the State Police Barracks. I met with Sergeant Ames who was doing desk duty. He set up a meeting for 10:00 a.m. the next morning.

Chapter Fifteen

Maine State Lt. Karl Moore, County Sheriff Sgt. Harry Monroe and Mill River Policeman Cyrus Hopkins were waiting in the Barracks when I arrived. I apologized for being late, explaining that I had received an early call from Abby. She told me that Pete had paid a visit to Miss Wood this morning. He gave his former teacher a bouquet of flowers. Abby said that he didn't go inside; just stood on the doorstep a few minutes talking with her.

We chatted about trivia for a few minutes, and then settled down. I had worked for and with all of them and felt right at home in the Barracks.

"Hannah, why don't you tell the guys what you told Sgt. Ames last night. We all need to be on the same wavelength."

I explained what had been going on at the Marshwood Federal Housing. It didn't take very long to go over the details. They all listened quietly and with interest until I finished.

Cyrus was the first to speak. "Then you think that Pete killed his mother and now plans on stealing Miss Wood's OC?"

"If I had any doubts whatsoever about this before, his visiting her this morning clinched it for me."

A lively discussion ensued. One by one they all agreed that I was right on target.

"You've put together a clear, concise case, Hannah. Good job!"

"I have a plan that I'd like to run by you guys."

They all laughed. Karl said, "Why doesn't that surprise us? We would have expected no less from you. Let's hear your plan."

My plan was a simple one and it didn't take me very long to tell them what I had in mind. "I'll move into the empty unit next to Miss Wood. I'll be an overweight, gray-haired, poorly dressed old woman. I'll be lame and walk with a cane. I'll furnish the place with a few things from my house. It shouldn't take long to catch Pete. If he's so addicted he'd kill his mother, he'll need Miss Wood's OC soon. I need listening equipment, with a recorder, mounted on the wall and a video camera mounted over the door. I have what I need to overcome Pete if it became necessary, but I would like permission for Abby to have some mace. I would supply it for her."

"Any questions?"

"Ayah, how do you plan on getting into the apartment?"

"Ah, I know where there's a key."

"Won't the management know you're there?"

"It's not likely since they seldom check on anything there. If they should show up they would just think I was supposed to be there."

"The, ah, cane. I assume it's the hollow one that you've put into service before?"

"Ayah."

"Ouch!"

"This will work, I know it will, and we'll get him for murder!"

They were quiet for a moment, and then the Lieutenant said, "It will be a hard sell with no evidence from the mother's apartment. He sure got everything out of it in a hurry!"

"Well, maybe not everything."

"Like what, Hannah?"

"When Abby and I went through the apartment, we didn't know if she was alive or not. I, ah – confiscated the mug from the bedroom. It had a small amount of liquid in it so I carefully wrapped it up and took it to Harding's Laboratory for an analysis. I figured that even if it wouldn't be any good in a court, it might scare Pete into a confession."

There was what seemed like a long spell of silence before the Lieutenant said, "You are something else, Hannah. Go ahead and put your plan into motion. Harry, get her what she needs, and send a grungy-looking repairman to attach the equipment she needs."

"When will you be there, Hannah?"

"Fairly early tomorrow, but I'll have the door unlocked real early, by 6:00 a.m."

"Good enough Hannah. I'll pick up the mug and the results from the lab."

"That's good, because it's there under your name."

"I would have expected no less from you, Hannah. Keep us up to speed via your cell phone. We're all glad to have you aboard on this one!"

"Ayah, and I'm glad you are with me – oh, as of tomorrow I'll be Dorcus Bailey. I'll use my old, unregistered pick-up and take the back roads to get there so that no one at the housing recognizes my vehicle."

"You're lucky you don't have to do this often, Han, ah, Dorcus. Cyrus would love to ticket you!"

We all were in really good spirits as we resumed our different, never easy, jobs.

Chapter Sixteen

"They approved of our plan, Abby. They need to be able to get in early in the morning to attach the listening device and put up a video camera. Can you get the door unlocked by 6:00 in the morning?"

"Sure can."

"Hopefully no one will see you."

"The only one up early is Dumpster Dan and I'll wait until he climbs into the dumpster before I unlock the door. Am I supposed to know you?"

"I think you should just treat me like you do the other people. You stop in to see and help everyone so one more won't make a difference. Just play it cool and check in once in awhile. Pete is obviously going to be suspicious of you, so you need to stay alert all the time. We can stay in close contact on the cell phones. And,

Abby, be sure to keep the mace with you all the time. The cops know I gave it to you."

"I will and I'll watch for anything unusual going on. Is someone going to help you move in?"

"Yes, I'll ask Fred, the guy who mows my lawns. I'm not bringing much, just my lounge chair to sleep in, a microwave, instant coffee, bread, peanut butter, jelly, plastic knives, forks and spoons, paper cups and napkins and a trash bag."

"Pete will probably be back in a day or two. He won't wait very long to start switching meds, if he hasn't already."

"Hopefully he hasn't or we'll have to wait until she needs her prescription refilled. Before it gets any later, I need to call Fred to make sure he can move me early tomorrow. See you around."

"OK, the door will be unlocked and I'll keep an eye on it until you get here."

"Good. Oh, I meant to tell you that my name will be Dorcus Bailey and I'm coming over in the old pick-up. Goodnight."

I called Fred and told him that I was working undercover on a case and no-one could know that I was there, and that the door would be unlocked for him to move my stuff inside. "Will you be able to help me?"

"I'd be glad to move your things before I go to work in the morning. I'll be anxiously waiting to find out just what you're up to this time."

I stood quietly looking out over the lake. The moon was up, the frogs were calling and a gentle breeze was pushing waves onto the sand. I felt my whole body begin to relax. I grabbed a quilt and headed for my couch on the screened porch, my favorite spot in the whole world to sleep.

Chapter Seventeen

Even the sounds of the frogs and the gentle splash of the waves on the sand didn't work to comfort me. I kept waking up all night, thinking of something else that I needed to take with me. I'd get up, add it to my list and lay back down.

What if I get someone hurt from doing this? I jumped at the sound of my voice! I can always self start myself by hearing my voice and I made myself get up and get moving. A long, hot shower followed with a mug of hot, black coffee helped me immensely. I began getting the things on my list ready for Fred to take them.

Fred arrived and quickly loaded my things into his pickup. "I'll stop here every day Hannah, to make sure everything is OK."

"Thanks, I'm taking my old pickup and I'll be Dorcus Bailey while I'm there. You can reach me on my cell phone if you need to. You have my number and know where the keys are."

"Ayah, take care."

He left and I began my makeover.

A long time ago, I went to a Halloween Masquerade Party sponsored by the Fall River Fire Department. My late husband had gone as a woman, Chiquita Banana; he had great looking legs! I went as an old, fat bag-lady. He won first prize for the women. Nobody knew that it was him, and they sure did tease him about his disguise! I didn't win anything but I saved both costumes.

I began taking my things out of the old trunk. I put the beige cotton stockings on first. I had lined them with cotton balls to make my legs look lumpy. Next I put on the blue cotton old dress that was two sizes too big and packed with extra material sewn into it in all the right places. One more item and I would be done. I got the old, out of shape tan sweater and put it on. It hung loosely and lopsided and was large enough to wrap around me. I tied it around my new, lumpish body. My heavily padded backside and sagging breasts completed this part of the costume.

I put on a pair of old run over shoes. They were badly in need of a polish. I loved those shoes and never could bear throwing them out. They were perfect for this job. Next was a long-haired, curly gray wig that had held up really well over the years. It needed to be combed. I didn't comb it! I plunked it on my head, making sure my real hair was totally covered up. Last, but not least, I added my black-rimmed glasses.

I picked up my cane and walked over to my full-length mirror to take a look. I was now a heavy old woman with no waistline and a stomach that hung low. Laughing at my reflection, I thought, *Nobody will recognize me. I don't even know who this is*!

I pumped the throttle on my old beat-up pickup truck and it started on the second try. I used this old junker a lot around my land and never bothered to update the plates. I wasn't too concerned. I knew all the back roads to get from here to there, and drove slowly to my new rent.

Chapter Eighteen

I chugged into the lower parking lot. There were no designated spaces so I went to the far end and parked.

I slid out of the pickup, got my purse, small suitcase on wheels, and the cane, and slowly limped towards the tarred path that dissected the lower units. To get to my unit, Number 14, from this lower side meant climbing a flight of wooden stairs. Abby's place was just before the stairs and as I passed in front of her window, she raised her thumb in an OK signal. Then she motioned toward her porch railing. There was an envelope taped to it and I pulled it off as I hobbled by, tucking it into a sweater pocket.

Holding onto the railing I slowly started up the stairs, looking over the area as a dweller rather than a visitor. Dragging my suitcase up the stairs was no easy task. The stair treads were difference heights and were so poorly constructed that I felt as if they were sinking into the dirt with every step. The railing also wobbled back and forth and I wondered if it was going to fall over on me. I also found out the hard way that the railing was full of splinters!

The only other way for anyone to get from the upper unit to the lower unit was to go out to the road and around to the parking lot on the lower side. The laundry room and a small recreation room were at the far end of the lower unit. This made no sense to me, but added to my determination to do something - anything - to fix this mess.

I figured that the Cleeve Construction Company that built this Federal Building probably used leftovers from other jobs. I decided that while I was living here I'd make a list of everything that wasn't done up to standards. This would give me something to do while waiting for Pete to get caught.

As I neared my unit, I casually looked up and noticed a video camera over the door. It looked very much like an over-the-door light. I tried to turn the knob, and it was locked. I reached into my pocket, opened the envelop and removed a key. I unlocked the door, went inside and locked it behind me. I would never ask Abby how she managed to get the key. I knew that she hid many things in her bra and no one would ever dare to ask her about it.

Looking around I noticed a listening device attached to the wall. Cyrus's man had put a TV stand against the wall below it. Wires ran from the device to a recorder that was on the stand. There was a box of disks on the table. He had left me a notepad with his cell phone number on it. He also left me a note.

"Dear Mom, I hope you will be comfortable here. Call me if you need anything. You know I will always be very close by. Love, Willy"

This note reminded me that I needed to let my real kids know I wasn't home. I called my son in Sebago and my daughter in Connecticut and left messages to use my cell phone number if they called me. I would be away for a short time. They are two of the greatest children I could ever ask for and they wouldn't be the least bit surprised to hear that I was 'working' on another case.

There was no way to call Sam, because when he was on a job he was out of touch. I tried not to think about him but he hadn't called me for quite a long time and I never really was able to learn how to stop worrying about him.

I pushed my lounge chair over towards the window, adjusted the view finder so I could see if anyone was 'visiting' my neighbor and turned the sound up enough to know if someone visited her. Then I got out my notebook and pen and began making a list of the problems here at the Federal Housing. Maybe I could figure out a way to get some improvements made.

Chapter Nineteen

I sat looking out the window mentally wondering what item I should start my list with. *Ha, get with it, Hannah; you should call Abby before you start a list. She probably has a list of her own.*

"Oh, yes, I have a list and I'll bring it up to you. I try to go around all the units two or three times a week. Nobody will think it's strange if I stop at a new tenant's place."

I watched her wheel herself out through her too-small exit and slowly go down the tarred path. She disappeared around the lower unit and reappeared as she left the parking lot and started up the road. Twenty minutes later she wheeled to a stop in front of Unit 14.

I opened my door and invited her inside. She expertly maneuvered through the outside doorway, with about a half inch leeway. She then had to make a 45 degree right turn, in an area just about the size of her wheelchair, and came through the next doorway into the living-dining room.

"Well, good morning, I just observed a problem with this place that will be at the top of my list."

"Good, this has never made any sense to me. Why would anyone make an entryway so small that the physically handicapped could hardly get through it? Oh, and be sure to add that there isn't a screen door, a storm door, or screen windows."

"Ayah, I will. Probably no insulation in any of the walls, either!"

"You got that right. It's cold here in the winter and hot, I mean really hot, in the summer. You can't even open the windows and there are no air conditioners. The units on the backside, like mine, get the sun much of the day and the heat is unbearable. I have a fan in every room but they only blow the hot air around!"

"Does the Housing Authority supply the fans for you Abby?"

"No way. If we want fans, we have to buy them ourselves."

Abby stopped talking and reached into the large bag that went everywhere with her. She passed me a covered cup of coffee, and then got one out for herself. Next came two home-made muffins.

"I saw how little Fred moved in for you and figured this would taste good."

"Will it ever! Thanks Abby, you're a wonderful friend."

She held up her cup, smiled and said, "To friendship!"

We sat quietly for a few minutes, enjoying this time and space.

"Someday I'd really like to know how you got a key that fits this unit."

"Someday, when I'm out of this hell hole, I'll tell you!"

"Good enough, now let's get down to business. I have already put those dangerous stairs on the list. I think they just set the railing stakes into the ground without securing them so they are very wobbly. The railing has splinter all over them and the steps are all different heights. Some of them slant toward the back and some slants so bad to the front that you wonder if you're going to slide right off them!"

"Good, you're right again, and if you can't go up and down stairs you have two other choices. You can go down the road and around the whole unit, like I do, or go down the grassy hill. Not very many of us use the hill; it gets real slippery when the grass is wet."

"The laundry and recreation room are at the far end of the lower unit, right?"

"Yes, and residents in the lower units can't go directly to them either. Why in the world would anyone make a nice level path along the front units and then make three steps to get from one side of the units to the other?"

"It makes no sense at all. Spend our Federal Tax money to build Elderly Housing and the elderly and handicapped can't get there from here!"

"None at all, Hannah. And in the winter nobody knows how to shovels or plow so it makes getting around even more difficult!"

"I remember when I lived across the street, they'd come with a big bucket loader, five men and two shovels. They were here all day, doing nothing!"

"You made our day that time when you were shoveling your driveway by hand and came over here. I don't know what you said to them, but they sure as hell started working. We loved you for that! What did you say, anyway?"

"Oh, I just asked them if they knew that my tax dollars paid for the bucket loader and that I was paying their salary. Since they weren't working I'd just borrow my bucket loader and take it over and clear the snow off my road with it! I started to climb up into it and the driver jumped up the other side into the seat."

"We're just having our coffee break!"

"Well, I've been out shoveling snow for an hour and none of you have done anything. Rather a long coffee break, don't you think?"

"All of a sudden everyone got really busy! I could feel their anger all the way back to my place!"

Abby burst out laughing. "Could you really drive that big rig?"

"Oh yes, when my Dad had his construction and logging business, I worked many of the ten to three shifts. I used a forklift to load the logs onto the trucks and drove the trucks to the lumber mills. I did this for two years during my junior and senior years in high school. I loved the job but when Dad went bankrupt and sold all his equipment, I was really relieved. It was tough work with little time to sleep."

We had finished the coffee and muffins, and I cleaned things up, throwing away any trash into a trash bag I brought with me.

"By the way, Abby, do you know who built this housing?"

"Ayah, the Cleeve Construction Company, who else? They owned the land and probably offered HUD a really good deal on it."

"Well, that figures. They had to bribe somebody to get the federal housing units moved from the lakeside to up here. Once you've got someone in your pocket, it's a given that you can then do any damn thing you want to."

"We've sure got a good start on the list and I don't want to stay too long. No need to draw attention to Unit 14! I'll be back later. Thanks, Hannah, I mean Dorcus!"

She maneuvered back outside and wheeled her way along to visit with the other tenants.

Chapter Twenty

It was a long, hot, boring day. I needed to keep busy so I worked on the research that I brought with me. I needed to find out all that I could about ghosts. My next book, *Tainted Town*, would include a haunted house that my family and I had lived in. Ayah, I know, you don't believe in ghosts! That's OK, I understand, neither did I 'til I lived with one!

The day dragged on. Not much was happening next door and as the sun moved toward the west the heat rose. Luckily the water here was pure and very cold. The developers had done something right! I kept a paper cup of water and a wet cloth close by. It helped now to cool me down enough to relax. I pushed the lounge chair into the recline position and dozed off.

The sun had sunk behind the lower units when a knock on my door woke me up. Abby was back, with dinner, and one of her fans! We sat quietly listening to the sounds of the fan and the movement next door. We ate hamburgers, potato chips and drank ginger ale. Then we got back to work.

"One of the biggest problems here is that HUD is now letting handicapped people like me into what was supposed to be housing for the elderly. This really causes a lot of problems!"

"I hadn't thought about that aspect, give me some examples?"

"Sure will. The physically handicapped, like me, only have to deal with the physical things, like units that don't accommodate us. But, it's the mentally handicapped residents that are really upsetting the senior citizens!"

"I can believe that; I wonder how HUD can get away with this"?

"I checked with them before I moved here. They told me that new laws prohibit them from discriminating against anyone. They cannot check into a person's background and/or get any information on what mental or physical problems an applicant has!"

"So they have to group young, old, physically and mentally disabled into a housing unit and to hell with the problems this creates!"

"Ayah, and we do have some problems!"

"And you're going to clue me in, right?"

"Right, I'll start with the latest tenant. Willy is mentally handicapped, probably 40 years old. He has the upper level end unit that is closest to the parking lot and road. Everyone has to go past his unit to go anywhere. Willy sits in a patio chair in his open doorway with no pants or underwear on!"

"An exhibitionist!"

"He sure is. He wears an undershirt that comes to his waist and nothing else. He also sits with his legs sprawled out. This is not something the elderly ladies, or anyone else, really wants to see every time they need to come and go somewhere!"

"An exhibitionist has an abnormal urge to expose his genitals. I can't believe that HUD couldn't get background information on him; he must have a long list of problems! Did you call HUD about this, Abby?"

"Ayah, I did. They said Willy had the right to sit naked in his doorway if he wanted to and nothing could be done to stop him!"

"Unreal, so according to them nothing can be done?"

"Well, I've been thinking that now that I have some mace, I could maybe threaten him into at least wearing underpants!"

"Don't do that, Abby, you'd just get into trouble and get kicked out!"

"Oh, sure, it would be me not him, right?"

"Yes, but before I leave I might just see what I can do! Find out all you can about him from the old ladies and tell them to go by him on the far side of the parking lot. Tell them not to look at him and try to ignore him. Exhibitionists are sexually deviant and they need to get attention from others!"

"I'll let all the ladies know what we're dealing with and get all the info I can for you."

"Great. What else do we need to add to my list Abby?"

"Well, I'm probably the only one that is bothered by Dumpster Dan. I'm the closest to the trash bin and it's terribly annoying to get woken up early every morning with him climbing into the trash bin. He throws stuff out and slams the doors when he's done picking the trash!"

"I sure wouldn't want to have him wake me up."

"Yes and his cat follows him there and sits by the bin loudly meowing all the time he's inside it!"

"Isn't he the one that stole your green underpants from the laundry room dryer?"

"Ayah, he's a weird one, maybe I could talk him into giving my panties to Willy to wear!"

"Well, I'm not sure that would work but Dumpster Dan is now added to my list. I don't believe we'll cure him but maybe we can get the trash bin moved. Let's look around for a better spot for it before I leave here."

"I better get back home before it gets dark. I'll sneak up here early in the morning with coffee and muffins again. Do you like corn or bran muffins best?"

"I like anything that is home cooked, as long as I don't have to cook it!"

"Thank you, Han, ah, Dorcus, I'm so thankful that you care about us. Goodnight."

I watched as Abby slowly wheeled out of sight.

Chapter Twenty-One

Sometime in the night I woke up. A plan on how to get better conditions for the Housing residents was bouncing around in my brain. I knew from past experience that I needed to get up and jot down the ideas. If I didn't do it now they would get lost somewhere in my head where they would disappear forever.

I scribbled them onto my notebook and went back to sleep. My cell phone ringing woke me up. Abby was on her way up with breakfast. After we ate, she listened and watched next door so that I could have a long, leisurely shower. Then we continued adding to our list.

"I guess the next thing that bothers me is the lack of ventilation for the kitchens and bathrooms. There are only two roof vents for 10 apartments, one at each end. All of our odors go into the crawl space over our ceilings.

"By law there has to be a vent for every bathroom."

"Sure, that's the law but look at the roof down below here, how many vents are coming out of the roof?"

"Two, and there are 10 units, I'd never noticed that before. The Code Enforcement Officer made darn sure that I had two vents for two bathrooms in my place."

"The back to back units are both vented into the same pipe, so the odor is even worse because we smell whatever comes from the unit behind us!"

"Ugh, that's not only smelly but potentially very harmful to your health!"

"Ayah, tell me about it, the man who lives behind me works at the Mill River Dump and he brings home his pick-up full of recyclable trash every day. He leaves it in the parking lot all the time and there's a rule that we can't leave any trash in or around our vehicles!"

"Another rule that doesn't get enforced. I'll add it to the list."

"The trash includes dead animals and road kill; he recycles them by cooking them every night. The odor that penetrates my unit is disgusting!"

"Have you complained about this?"

"Oh, yes, and would you believe that the gentleman has the right to cook anything he wants to? So, I put a tinfoil barrier behind my vent. It keeps the odor out of my place, but I have to take it off whenever I fry anything, and then put it back again."

"Good for you!"

"Ayah, but if they find out I'll have to take it off. Against the rules you know."

"It almost sounds as if everyone but you can do what they want to do. Somehow I'm going to find a way to change this place!"

"I'll be behind you the whole way, Dorcus!"

"Meantime, there has to be something we can do. Who lives in the Unit that backs up to the storage shed?"

"Dumpster Dan does, why?"

"Maybe you can talk the Mill River Dump scrounger into taking Dumpster Dan with him every day. Tell him he can make a lot more money on the trash he brings home. Then tell him he needs to start cooking his road kill at

Dumpster Dan's place. You have a friend in the State Sanitation Department and you're going to get him kicked out of this place if he doesn't cooperate."

"Wow, Dorcus, this just might work!"

"If it doesn't, then I'll get a lawyer on behalf of the tenants here and watch the guys at HUD squeal on their benefactor, the Cleeve brothers!"

"All right! Good for you! Way to go!"

"Now, you better get out of here before our friend Pete arrives. I have a feeling that we won't have to wait much longer for him to run out of OC."

The day seemed to drag on forever. The heat was oppressive and nothing in the whole place seemed to be moving at all, except the fan!

I called a friend in the State Abuse Division and asked for a favor. She said she would check and call me back. Then I worked on my research, alternating it with my growing plan on how to make life better in this place. A few hours later my friend called me and I had the information I needed. "No-pants" had a long background of indecent exposure and had served time. He was still on probation but she doubted that HUD would even try to make a complaint. "They have their rules that they have to go by you know!"

I thanked her for the information and began to figure out how to best deal with this pervert!

Chapter Twenty-Two

The next morning Abby had arrived with breakfast and gone by the time the video camera showed Pete coming down the walkway. I quickly checked the recording equipment, and then called Cyrus.

"Good, Hannah, I've been sitting close by and figured he was heading there. I'll put a call in for backup. We'll have a blockade set up at the foot of the hill. If he's got the OC on him, we'll nail him for good!"

"If he sees you, he'll throw it out the window."

"Ayah, I'll have some men stationed in spots down the mountain. They'll know if he tries that."

"Will you let me know when you've got him?"

"Sure will Hannah, and if we find it on him, I'll send a man to take the video camera and recording."

"Great, I have something I need to take care of in the morning, so I'll be here all night."

A short time later Cyrus stopped by. "We got him, Hannah. He did throw the stuff out the window. We got a picture of this and had no trouble getting the vial of OC. He rammed into one patrol car but it slowed him down enough for the rest of us to nail him. We'll keep him in the local jail overnight so we can have plenty of time to question him.

He's going to really be hurting when he can't get more OC into him; I wouldn't want to be in his shoes!"

"Can you get a new prescription of meds for Miss Wood?"

"Hadn't thought about that, but since we need the other for evidence, I'll send someone to take care of this."

"Great, guess I can move on and out of here tomorrow."

Abby was waiting at the end of the walkway and wheeled to my unit.

"I brought back your mace."

"Thanks. I'm glad you didn't need it."

"I was hiding out behind some cars in the lower parking lot. I can't wait to hear what happened."

I told her the whole story and how I planned to deal with Willy in the morning. She agreed to check him out every day to make sure he had his pants on. We sat in silence for awhile, enjoying the results of our plan.

"Do you think I should check in on Miss Wood before the cop come?"

"That's a good idea, Abby, she knows you and if she didn't know what happened she might be really upset to have a cop visit her."

"OK, will I see you in the morning?"

"I sure hope so; I've gotten kind of spoiled having my breakfast brought to me. I may stay here until 'they' catch me."

"Ha, you could probably be here forever!"

"You got that right. I'll see you in the morning."

Chapter Twenty-Three

Abby arrived early with breakfast one more time. We sat quietly for awhile enjoying our successful plan to catch Pete.

"How did Miss Wood take the news?"

"She's a feisty one. First she was really mad to think she'd trusted Pete, then thrilled to be what she called a lead player in our plot."

"Abby, do you know if these outside walls have been insulated?"

"I haven't checked, but I'll bet you a shore dinner they haven't any at all!"

"I'll take the bet, now let's find out. I have a flat bar in the pickup. I'll go get it and meet you at your place."

We carefully removed the molding off one side of the living room picture window.

"Well, that doesn't prove much. We can't see where any has been stapled but we really need to see behind the sheetrock."

"No problem, I'll cut a small section out."

Before I could tell her not to, she had a small chunk of it cut out. She turned and grinned at me. "Don't worry, I can patch it back in!"

We took turns checking out the opening. No insulation. Surprise, surprise!

"OK, we need to start by getting pictures of this and everything else that's been done wrong."

"Ayah, and that's right up my alley. I can do that. Let's make a list of what I need to video so I won't forget anything."

"Good, I'll come back over with my video camera for you."

OK, here's the list:

This hole with no insulation in it

The solid unventilated picture window

The small entryway and the size of the doors

No screen doors

The vent over the stove

"Maybe I can get Dan to take his vent cover off and I'll try for a picture that really shows that it's all just one. Maybe I can put a yardstick through and get pictures from both sides."

"That's a good idea, Abby."

"If he won't help, I'll find two other back-to-back tenants who will. OK, back to the list."

The roof showing only two vents for 10 units

The wobbly stairs leading up to the upper units

Abby laughed. "I bet I can get someone to push the railing to show how wobbly it is!"

"That's another good idea."

The steps on the front of the lower units where there should be a ramp

No screen doors

No screens for the windows

Windows that won't open

"I'll bet Miss Wood would love to help me, I'll even video how you have to get a stretcher out of here."

"Great, Abby. With all this evidence, I'll have enough to take to the State Victim Advocate and the Attorney General. The

Cleeve brothers aren't going to get away with fraud this time!"

"I bet we can get everybody here enthused about this. We all need to have something to work on to make living here better!"

Our conversation was interrupted when Fred arrived to take my things back to the Lake. He refused to take the money I had for him. "Hannah, you've done so much to help me; let me help you now."

I gave him a hug and he left to load up his truck.

"I have to go now but I'll be back as soon as I can with the video camera. By the way, I'm going to ride up to the upper level and have a little discussion with Willy before I leave."

Abby smiled, gave me a hug and a "Thank you" and I headed for my truck.

Chapter Twenty-Four

Willy was sitting, naked and spread-eagled in his doorway, staring off into the woods. I put my camera strap over my shoulder, and got out of the truck, limping and using my cane.

"Morning Willy."

"Who's you?"

"Someone that's going to get you sent back to the mental ward."

"I ain't done nothin'."

"Yes you have, Willy. You know the rules and you've broken them, so back you go!"

"You can't make me!"

I took a picture of him.

"Why'd you do that?"

"For evidence, Willy."

"You're a bitch, old lady; get to hell out of here. You can't make me move!"

"You see this, Willy? It's called mace and it would smart something fierce if you got some of it sprayed on your genitals! I'm going to leave it here with some of the ladies you've abused by sitting here naked."

"That stuff's against the law."

"So are you, Willy."

"I'm a free man, I can do any damn thing I want to, so get lost, you ugly witch!"

"You just threatened me, Willy!"

I pointed my cane at him, clicked the button on the side of it and a five inch dagger snapped out of the bottom.

"Holly shit, what did you do that for?"

"To scare you enough to believe that I'm serious, Willy. You're a sexual exhibitionist and a sick excuse for a man!"

"Go to hell, bitch!"

"You stop sitting here exhibiting your manhood or you could suddenly have no manhood to exhibit!"

Willy jumped up, knocking his chair over, and fled into his apartment. I heard the lock snap into place.

I returned to the truck, climbed in and sat quietly to let my heart beat slow down. This is such a horrific disease, with so little hope for a cure! I thought of all the sexual abusers that I had helped put in jail. I always had to deal with my feelings of sadness and sympathy, mingled with my contempt for them!

I turned the key and drove very slowly over the back roads to home.

Chapter Twenty-Five

I gave Abby the video camera. We sat outside silently, enjoying the morning sun that beamed down on us, sort of like welcoming us to a new day. The birds were busy gathering food and the bald eagles watched us from their big old nest high in their pine tree.

Abby interrupted the tranquility. "I'd love to be a bird."

"A cardinal?"

"No, I think I'd rather be an eagle. I wouldn't ever have to depend on humans to feed me; I'd be strong and healthy and soar everywhere!"

"You're going to be able to do everything one of these days and without being an eagle."

"Ayah, you really make me believe that I can do that, Hannah."

"How were things here last night?"

102

"Lots going on. First a State car came, then an ambulance, then a truck and our problem in the upper level first unit is no more!"

"That's good!"

"Are you going to tell me how you managed all that?"

"I don't think so. I'm not proud of what I did. It makes me so damn angry that we pay taxes to the State who hire idiots to make laws, some of them stupid laws that help no one and harm so many!"

"Ayah, I know just how you feel!"

"I'm sorry, Abby. I didn't mean to sound off to you. For God's sake, you're a victim, I can't tell you anything you don't already know!"

"Oh, but you can. So many of us just sit here day after day complaining and doing nothing about it. You've been here a few days and you've changed our misery and self pity into hope and determination!"

"Is Miss Wood going to help you with the videos?"

"You bet she is and she's not alone. The sun was barely up this morning before the news spread that Pete was arrested for murdering his mother and stealing Miss Wood's medicine, and that Willy had moved out during the night."

"Good news travels fast around here!"

"It sure does. Miss Wood also told everyone that she was going to help me video all the problems in this housing and most of them want to help."

"That's great; she is really good at getting them all involved!"

"Ayah, she wants to set it all up ahead of time, making sure everyone has something to say."

"You are all taking a giant step away from being victims. Maybe when I get an appointment with the State Victim Advocate, I'll rent a bus and you all can go with me."

"That's a great idea, Hannah. What an impact that would have!"

"And if we have to, we'll all go to the Attorney General 'cause we're going to get this Housing fixed!"

"Way to go, Hannah. I'll pass the news around. I bet most of them will want to be there."

I spent the rest of the day on the computer compiling information and coming up with an official-looking Problem Document to the Attorney General, from the Residents of the Marshwood Federal Housing on Mickmash Mountain in the town of Mill River, Maine. and explained that we would like an appointment with him. At that time we would bring a video that would attest to the problems on the list.

I wrote a cover letter and faxed a copy of this and the document to the State of Maine Victim Advocate. I asked for him to set up an appointment for all of us with the Attorney General as soon as possible.

Before the day was over, we had received a reply. We had an appointment for next Wednesday, at 11 am. with the Victim Advocate. He would be representing the Attorney General at this meeting. I called Abby with the good news. I knew that it wouldn't take long for her to spread the word to all the others.

Chapter Twenty-Six

Miss Wood immediately reverted back to being a teacher. She called for a meeting of all the residents in the recreation room. She had decided that the group would present their iniquities in the form of a series of vignettes. Each of the ladies living there would have the chance to participate in the program.

"Now you know that you don't have to help with this, but I dearly hope that you all will want to. All that you have to do is read something that I'll write. Each of you will give a short verbal description of a gross problem that you have had to live with."

"I have written an opening statement and I think that Abby should be the person to read it." She passed the statement to Abby.

"Thank you, Miss Wood, I'll be glad to."

"Let it be known that we, the residents of the Marshwood Towers Federal Housing hereby declare that we will no longer tolerate living in a sub-standard environment. We are submitting the following video which contains a series of vignettes describing the insufferable conditions we are forced to subsist under. We request that our voices be heard and that our rights be honored by your office. We need you to initiate for us a class action suit against the Cleeve Construction Company, charging them with fraud and endangerment perpetrated upon us."

Everyone was quiet for a few minutes, and then they clapped and cheered!"

"I have written each vignette based on the list Abby and Hannah had made. Each of you will get a copy of your part in this drama."

She gave everyone their copy and Abby began their production.

I had been invited to attend this performance and I had a wonderful day, tagging along with the crew and watching with amazement as these former submissive human beings transformed into articulate, compassionate and tenacious champions for justice.

My pride in this group was matched by their pride in themselves and each other. There was instant camaraderie in a group which up to this day seldom talked to each other, except for maybe saying, "Hello."

We gathered in the small community room and watched their movie. There were some suggestions made but I talked them into leaving it just as it was. The final vignette was the video of Abby trying to get a stretcher out of her unit. It was an amazing demonstration of one of their worst problems, guaranteed to get results. The facts and their sincerity came through loud and clear and that's what would impress the powers that be.

I paused for a moment, then grinned and said, "Oh, I guess I forgot to tell you that I've hired a bus and we're all going to the State Capital in Augusta next Wednesday to meet with the State Victim Advocate who will be representing the Attorney General. I sure hope you all can go!"

There were smiles, laughter and yelps of "You bet" and "I'll be there" and clamor mixed with discussing "what will I wear" and "I'll have to have my hair done." And then they were quiet and some were crying.

"This is a phenomenal event for all of us. You have given us the chance to regain our dignity and respect for ourselves and each other, Hannah. Because of you we are now working together for the good of all of us, and with you and Abby to lead the way, we'll be on that bus next Wednesday, raring to get justice for all of us."

"Thank you, Miss Wood, but I couldn't have done any of this alone. Abby and you are the heroes here."

"Well, I don't know about that but I know what I want to do now. She went over to the archaic upright piano and hunted around until she found what she was looking for, the shabby old *Reader's Digest Family Song Book*. She plunked down on the piano bench, opened the song book to page 58 and began playing *Happy Days Are Here Again*.* We all gathered around and sang along with her.

Happy Days Are Here Again, from *The Reader's Digest Family Song Book* ©1969.

EVORA JORDAN

Published by The Reader's Digest Association, Inc.

Chapter Twenty-Seven

The clutter that I had amassed while doing research was right where I had left it – strewn all over the dining room table. I needed to get all of this organized and filed, but I was restless. I knew that I needed to get away from my work, away from worrying about Abby, ayah, and Sam. If he was killed would I ever know? Probably not, but I've known this all along.

OK, enough already! I jumped at the sound of my voice. When I get to the point where I'm talking to myself, I know exactly what to do to regain control.

I made a peanut butter and strawberry jam sandwich on whole wheat bread. I put on my bathing suit and sneakers, grabbed a towel, a bottle of water and a Tony Hillerman book. A few minutes later I was peddling my paddle boat along the shore of the lake.

Down the lake apiece there was a point of land that jutted out, separating my cove from the next one. Tall pines and large boulders had kept the Girl's Camp owners from building anything this far away from their main buildings. As I rounded the point I stopped peddling and coasted toward a shallow, sandy niche between two of the boulders. I back-peddled the boat into my hideout.

I love to read, it has always been my preferred escape from reality. I spent the rest of the day with Hillerman's favorite character, Officer Jim Chee of the Navajo Tribal Police.

The sun was hanging low over the lake and the wind now was coming out of the north, making my trip home easier and faster. I dragged the boat back to its stand and a short time later was peacefully sleeping on my front porch couch.

Chapter Twenty-Eight

I got up as usual with the sun. It was way too early to call anybody so I swam the cove and back and sat for a short time enjoying the lake. By the time I finished my two cups of hot, black coffee and toast, I was ready to get this day moving. I called Philip Peabody, the Director of the Mill River Hospital and asked for an appointment to meet with him.

"I'll be glad to meet with you, Hannah. I hope there's no problem?"

"I hope there isn't too Phil, but there's something I think I should discuss with you. I'd rather wait until we meet to explain further."

"You still the early bird?"

"Oh, yes!"

"Good, How about joining me for breakfast in my office about 8:30 tomorrow?"

"Thanks Phil, sounds like a plan. See you then."

I started to call the Mickmash Bus Company but decided to take a ride there instead. Many of the employees were former students of mine and I always enjoyed seeing them. I wanted to explain to them in person why and when I needed to rent a bus and driver.

I drove slowly around the lake and then took the main drag to the New Hampshire border. It was hot, one of our dog days when the heat seemed to penetrate everything. It was muggy even when I got closer to the foothills of the White Mountains. I wanted to stop by one of the mountain streams to cool off, but I was beginning to be a little concerned!

There had been a car behind me most of the way. If I went faster, it did and if I slowed down it also slowed down! I fully expected that interfering in both the murder of Susan and the problems at Marshwood wouldn't go unnoticed by the Cleeve brothers! If I had to make a guess, I'd say they did know! Would they have someone following me around?

Ayah! Were they? I'd better find out!

Relying on my Crisis Intervention Training received when I helped organize the 3rd Rape Counseling Hotline, I locked my doors and watched for the first safe place to stop!

For the next two miles I alternated going fast, then slow, and my follower did the same! I knew there was a filling station down the road apiece and a short time later I pulled off the road and up to a full service pump.

My 'tail', in a beat up green Ford pick-up, passed by and pulled off the highway. He sat there with his blinker on and I jotted down his license plate number!

A teenager came out and filled my gas tank, washed my windows, filled my windshield washer and checked my oil. I'm spoiled, I love full service! While he was working on my car, I dialed the Bus Company. As I figured, one of my students, Billy, answered. I told him there might be a problem and gave him the license number.

"I'll be glad to check that for you Mrs. G. We got a good crew here now, and will be waiting right here for you, shouldn't be more than ten more minutes. Now be sure not to look at him when you go by, might make him a little leery! Oh, jeez Mrs. G, you already know all about that stuff!"

"Ayah Billy, but it does my heart good to know that you know it too. See you shortly!"

I paid for the gas, tipped the attendant and pulled away from the gas tanks. My heart was pounding and I began sweating. Just how far would the Cleeve's go to get me off their backs? I knew that I needed to just sit here for a few minutes until I calmed down I finally pulled back onto the road. I passed the pickup without looking at it, and drove the speed limit to the Bus Terminal. The green pickup kept going and shortly pulled off the road. Billy came out and opened my car door, helping me out. I locked the car and we walked inside together.

"I got the information you wanted, Mrs. G. The pickup belongs to Tom LaBlanc."

"I don't know anyone by that name, so I guess I probably don't need to worry about him."

"I know him. He's a no-good drunk and he does odd jobs off and on for The Cleeve Construction Company."

"Well, that puts an entirely different slant on matter."

"How so, Mrs. G?"

"Well, without going into the whole story, I'm here to rent a bus and driver for next Wednesday. The destination is the State Capitol for a meeting with our State Victim Advocate. I'm taking a bus full of tenants who live at the Marshwood Federal Housing. We're asking for help in getting some badly needed repairs done, possibly pursuing a class action suit if that's what it takes to get results!"

"Don't tell me, let me guess." Marshwoods was built by The Cleeve Construction Company."

"Right on, Billy, I always knew you had a good head on your shoulders."

"You aren't going to let that fellow in the pickup stop you from going are you?"

"No way. We'll just have to be more watchful and careful!"

"Give me a few minutes, Mrs. G. I'll do the paper work and be right back."

I watched out the window at the green pickup. He had turned it around, obviously anticipating my return to Mill River.

Billy returned and his brother, Jimmy, was with him.

"Hi, Mrs. G, good to see you."

"Good to see you too, Jimmy. I can't believe you guys are all grown up; it doesn't seem that long since I was trying to teach you history."

"You never gave up on us. You always told us to try to do the best we could no matter what we were doing."

"Ayah, and you both did really good."

"Everything's in place for next Wednesday. Jimmy and I are both going with you. We'll come to Marshwoods and pick you all up. What time do you need to be in Augusta?"

"By 11:00 a.m., Billy, but how come both of you are going?"

"One to drive and one to watch our tail, Mrs. G, and we've swapped our day off so we can take you. The bus will cost you but we're going for free."

"You don't have to do that."

"We want to and we bet that we're going to learn a lot while we're at it. So don't give us any grief."

"OK, I won't but thank you both very much. I better head back home. See you Wednesday."

"Don't worry if you see an old beat up black car following the green pick-up, Mrs. G. I'm going to make sure you get home safe."

I smiled, gave them both a hug, and went out to lead the parade back to Mill Town.

The parade ended in the parking lot of our only bank. The green pickup keep going and Billy followed me, pulling in beside my CRV.

"Thanks, Billy, we'll be waiting at the lower parking lot by 8:00 a.m., OK?'

"Sure is, see you then."

Chapter Twenty-Nine

I locked the car doors and waited a short time in the bank's parking lot. Nothing seemed out of place and I needed to get a few groceries. I went to the Mill River IGA store and wandered through all the aisles. No one seemed the least bit interested in me and I paid for my things and went back to my car. There was a paper tucked under my windshield wiper. The only thing on the paper was the word, BITCH! I removed the message, folded it up and put it in my purse. I might need this as evidence if this stupid harassment continued.

I headed back to the lake. I needed a good nights sleep before my meeting in the morning and I needed to call Abby before I went to bed.

Everyone knew where I lived and I kept glancing in the rear-view mirror. Nobody had followed me and I drove into the garage, and locked the doors behind me.

I called Abby. "Everything's taken care of. The bus will pick us up at 8:00 a.m. next Wednesday at your lower parking lot."

"Great, Hannah, thanks for calling."

"Abby, don't alarm the others, but someone followed me to the Bus Company and back today. They also left a sign under my windshield wiper that said, BITCH! I think whoever did this works for the Cleeves. I can't believe they would try to intimidate any of you, but be very watchful. Use your own good judgment as to whether or not you say anything to the others."

"Sure thing, Hannah, but I really believe that if they try anything it would only make all of use more determined than ever!"

"Good. Want to go to lunch tomorrow after my meeting at the hospital?"

"Why don't you stop off here? I'll fix lunch."

"Will do. Goodnight."

Chapter Thirty

I parked in the employee's lot behind the hospital. Philip's office was on the second floor and I went through the back entrance and took the stairs rather than the elevator. The fewer personnel that saw me here, the better!

Philip's door was open and he stood up as I looked into his office.

"Good Morning, Hannah, come in and have a seat. Good to see you!"

I closed the door and pushed a chair up close to his desk. He had coffee and fruit on it and he moved them close enough for me to help myself.

"I'm anxious to hear why you're here, Hannah!"

"I'll get right to the point, Phil. An elderly woman at the Marshwood Towers had a

122

son who had been stealing his mother's OC, substituting it with Entrie Coated Aspirin.

"That rots, Hannah, but how does this affect my hospital?"

"Each time this happened she would get really sick from taking the wrong medicine and call the Rescue Unit. They would bring her to your Emergency Unit."

"That's what they're supposed to do!"

Phil is a big man, slightly overweight but tall enough to carry it around. He always wears a white shirt and a navy blue tie. He was really good at this job and he knows it, but at this moment he was not a smiling, happy camper! I could see that he was quite annoyed; his face had turned a deep shade of red.

"I don't think I'm going to enjoy hearing what's next, but I have to. Tell me the rest of the story!"

"Each time she came here she would be treated and given a new prescription for OC, and each time her son would be called to pick her up. Her son would get the prescription filled, buy more Entrie Coated Aspirin, take his mother home, and switch the meds and leave."

"You know this for sure?"

"A friend of mine who lives at the housing followed the ambulance one day. Then she waited on a side street until Pete arrived and left. She followed them to the pharmacy and back home."

"Do you have proof of this?"

"She compared the medicine with the OC another resident had but nobody ever witnessed him swapping the pills."

"Then you don't know if that is what really happened, right?"

"A few weeks ago, Abby told her friend and the woman told her son that she was going to call the police. The last time he visited she ended up dead!"

"Is this being investigated by the authorities?"

"I don't have all the answers, Phil, but I'm here because one of the questions I did have was how someone could be brought to your hospital time and time again, get a prescription for narcotics, and nobody noticed how frequently it happened."

He leaned back in his chair and took a few deep breathes.

"I don't understand that either, Hannah, and I'm the person who is supposed to know everything that goes on here."

"I know that, Phil, that's why I felt I needed to tell you this."

We both sat quietly, thinking and sipping coffee.

"My God, Hannah, this is not something that's easy to believe. If I didn't know you so well, I'd think you'd made it up to put into one of your murder mysteries. But it's real?"

"Yes."

He stood up, paced around a bit and came around his desk.

"First, I need to thank you for coming to me with this."

"Second, I want to let you know that I'll get to the bottom of what's going on here that would allow something like this to happen."

"Third, I'll meet with all the pharmacists in the area to make sure they are up to speed on what's happening. Pete must have been switching pharmacies each time or they would have caught on to what he was doing."

"Fourth, is there anything else you know but haven't told me?"

"Well, I did help in setting up a sting operation and Pete was caught in the act of stealing OC from an other woman. He's either behind bars now or in the detox infirmary at the jail."

"If this was to go public and we didn't know about it, we all could have lost our licenses!"

"Yes, I know. That's why I felt I had to tell you."

Phil had been pacing back and forth as we talked. Now he stopped and sat back down. He picked up his phone, dialed a number and barked, "I need to see you in my office, immediately!"

He began making notes and murmured, "I need to call the other area hospitals."

I stood up, picked up my purse and quietly left his office. I'm sure that he wasn't aware that I had left.

Chapter Thirty-One

I felt totally drained of energy and really only wanted to get back to the lake and space out for the rest of the day, but I had to be at Abby's for lunch.

I looked around the parking lot and went across to my CRV. I got in and sat there trying to decide what the next best way was to chill out. Ha, it didn't take me very long. I'd go shopping at Reny's, a small discount store that you can only find in Maine!

I love all the Reny's Stores but the Reny's in the coastal town of Belfast played a prominent role in *Tainted Sand*, my true murder book, and I have a real special connection to that store and to the town.

You can find anything you want or need at Reny's and for less money than anywhere else. Today I didn't buy anything but I very effectively freed my mind of any and all my problems.

Abby had hamburgers and a salad almost ready when I arrived. We went outside to eat, sitting under the shade of the only tree around, an apple tree, that was big enough to shade anything. Soon Dumpster Dan's cat showed up, meowing for his share.

"Oh, seeing the cat reminds me of something I need to tell you."

Abby was grinning from ear to ear.

"I've talked to both Dumpster Dan and the Trash Man and they went bonkers over your idea." When I left them they were discussing their new partnership. One more problem solved, thanks to you, Hannah."

"That's great, Abby, you're really good at arbitration."

"Everything has been very normal here so far. There's a little more activity from the women, and that's really good. No strangers and no Cleeve employees have been around."

"That's good news, I'm glad you're here to keep tabs on everything!"

"I'm glad I'm here too. The whole place seems so upbeat right now that it sure does help my disposition."

"I can't believe that the Cleeves would be stupid enough to cause any more trouble, but we do need to stay alert."

"They are driving by here much slower than they used to. If they think that bothers us, they are sadly mistaken! We always worried that they would hit one of our animals!"

"Or one of you."

"Right!"

We finished lunch and sat for a spell watching and listening to all the birds. They were so busy all the time; it sort of made you tired just watching them. They were not happy to have a cat around and gave him such a hard time that he gave up and left.

Abby laughed. "Too bad it wasn't as easy to get rid of unwanted people."

We heard a kik – ik – ik – ik, kleek – kleek – kleek sound and looked up at the mountain. The bald eagle was watching us from her huge nest in the big old pine tree.

Abby answered with her imitation of the call. I always get chills down my spine when I hear her 'talking' with the eagles. She sounds so much like them that it is really uncanny listening to her.

I got up, took the leftovers inside and put things back where they belonged. I washed what few dishes there were and got ready to leave for home.

"I'll leave you two old birds to yourself now. Stay safe."

Chapter Thirty-Two

The screened front porch is my preferred spot to get myself back on track. I got a bottle of water from the refrigerator and plunked down in my favorite lounge chair. It didn't take me very long to begin mentally organizing all the things I needed to do. As the list got longer I admonished myself.

Write it down, Hannah, or you'll forget what you're thinking.

I dutifully reached for my notepad and pen.

Top priority was that I needed to stay in touch with the Marshwood ladies. I was confident that Abby and Miss Wood could and would deal with any problems that arose between now and our trip. However, I knew that they might need a few pats on the back.

I was also toying with the idea of having a victory party for the group. I would need a theme for the party. I sat for awhile, gazing out across my front lawn. I'd planted lots of yellow and brilliant red day lilies, and red, yellow and white rose bushes. They shared their space with the wild flowers. Purple bellflowers, blue flags and deep pink swamp roses were growing everywhere. They were at their peak color now and were absolutely beautiful!

The colorful front yard gave me an idea; the theme would be flowers. Everyone could come to the party dressed as a flower! I'd make up a flower song quiz and think up something neat for the winner. Since this would be a celebration, maybe I'd give them a bottle of champagne. I would also give each of them a beautiful red rose.

I needed to decide what we would have to eat. Maybe I'd cook! I must be out of my mind, I don't like to cook! I do make great meatballs and tomato sauce. I'd only have to add some Italian bread, a tossed salad, cold drinks and ice cream. I'd probably just buy plastic utensils, and paper plates, some with flowers on them.

Ayah, I think I just talked myself into cooking up a party.

I went out to the kitchen and dug out my *Hannah Gray's Cook Book*, looked up meat in the index and opened to page 24. I wrote down everything I would need and put the note into my pocketbook. I would buy everything I needed later.

Well, I guess I had just worked myself out of the doldrums.

I called Abby to get her reaction to my plan.

"What a great idea, Hannah! Your parties are so much fun but let me help. I'll do the cooking!"

"You don't have to do that."

"It only makes sense to cook it here. You can buy what I'll need and I'll get Miss Wood to help organize everything! On top of that, I know that you really don't like to cook."

"You're absolutely right about that; you've convinced me. I've made a list of what I need to buy, and I'll pick up everything and bring it over."

"That's great; you know I love to cook!"

"Yes, I know, and if you and Miss Wood organize the party, it would be a big help also."

"We sure will, and we'll spread the news. This is going to be a great way to help us keep busy and avoid getting panicky about Wednesday's trip."

I hung up and wandered around the house. Then I went outside and wandered around out there. Everything was so peaceful and beautiful. I began to really relax as I pulled a few weeds away from the flowers.

I needed to get some exercise and decided to go for a walk. I went back to the house, grabbed a plastic bag, my cell phone and a bottle of water. I cut across the lawn to the old back camp road.

All of the summer folk were still here and I stopped to chat with any that were out and about. I was the only flatlander and year round person on this cove and as such was the designated winter guardian of their properties. It was a job I gladly took on; it helped get me outside in the cold weather.

Most of the time there were no problems, especially when the lake wasn't frozen over. Lake traffic picked up when the ice got thick enough for the snowmobilers to ride around on it. They tended to use any cleared space to get from their vehicles onto the lake.

Periodically I'd put my snowshoes on and check out the camps. I'd never found anything damaged but it was a good excuse to get me out and moving!

The weather had turned cooler today and everybody was either inside or away. I walked to the end of the road and cut across the lawn of the last camp. I took off my sneakers and returned home via the sandy cove.

There was always some debris that washed into the cove. I generally filled a plastic bag full of tennis balls, beer bottles, paper trash, cigarette butts, used condoms and many other discarded things. It was one of those frustrating things that I knew I couldn't ever stop people from doing. Today was no exception and I strolled along the cove, wading in water up to my ankles and filled up my bag.

Chapter Thirty-Three

With only one more day before the bus trip to Augusta, I knew I needed to keep busy. Worrying about how the day would turn out wouldn't help anyone. I called Abby.

"How's everything going over there?"

"Just great, Miss Wood and I think we should have the party on Thursday. Everyone will be busy today getting costumes ready and they won't have time to fret tomorrow."

"I just had the same thought. I'll pick up all the things this morning and drop them off to you."

"Good, I'll get the meatballs and sauce cooking today."

"See you soon."

I made a fast trip to the grocery store, bought what I needed and headed for Marshwood Towers. I was heading up the mountain, almost to the sharp curve, when a truck came speeding around the corner on my side of the road!

Instinct took over and I jerked the steering wheel to the left. The CRV tipped up on its two left wheels. I jerked it back to the right and it settled back to the road. I missed the truck, but only by inches!

During these few seconds I took a quick glance at the truck. Clarence was the driver and he was laughing. When I looked in my rear view mirror, he had disappeared down the hill and onto the highway.

I continued up the road, parked in the lower lot and sat shaking all over. There was no way he could have known that I'd be in that spot at that time! However, that wasn't what bothered me as much as how pleased he seemed to be. If he had hit me head on, we probably both would have been seriously hurt, maybe even killed!

I muttered to myself, *What kind of maniac would be laughing at something like this?*

I answered, *Probably a morning drunk on his way for more alcohol.*

All the things had been thrown out of the bags and tossed around the car. I got out and checked them. Nothing had broken and I repacked them and carried them up the path.

Abby met me at the door and insisted on taking two of the bags. She wheeled into the kitchen with them and started putting things in the refrigerator. I followed with the other bag, sat it on the counter and tears starting rushing down my cheeks.

"What's the matter, Hannah? You look ghastly. Let's go sit down in the living room. Are you alright?"

I made it to a chair, pawed through my pockets and found a tissue and wiped my face. Abby passed me a glass of water.

"Thanks, Abby, I just came very close to getting killed!"

"My God, what happened?"

I drank some water, took a few deep breaths and told her what happened.

"Those no good bastards! One of these days one or both of them are going to get someone killed!"

"When I looked at Clarence he was laughing like an idiot."

"He's a real loser; he and Clayton both ride this road as if they were the only ones on it. Are you sure that you're okay?"

"Yes, better now, thanks. I'll head back home. I want to get a Music Quiz written for Thursday."

"I can help with that, Hannah, you don't look so good!"

"Thanks, but I'll be fine and I'd much rather spend the rest of the day doing that than the cooking."

"You're so funny, Hannah. I love telling people that you wrote a cook book and you really don't like to cook!"

"Ayah, just plain crazy and glad I'm still alive to laugh about it."

"I'm glad too. Take it easy driving home."

"Thanks, Abby. I will"

I had to force myself to open the car door. I still felt shaky and I didn't know if I would be able to get in and drive home! I took a deep breath, yanked the door open, got in and turned the key. A few minutes later I slowly drove out of the parking lot and headed down the hill.

Twenty minutes later I hit the garage door opener, pulled into the garage and shut the door behind me. I sat for what seemed like a very long time. I was thankful that my CRV responded so well and that I still had the ability to think fast, real fast. I was also thankful that I was alive to be upset about what happened!

I guess it just wasn't my time to die!

I felt drained of all my energy. I reached for my purse and slowly got out of my vehicle. I went into the house, walking, stumbling really, out to the porch. I collapsed onto the couch, pulled my quilt over me, closed my eyes and went to sleep.

Chapter Thirty-Four

The sound of my cell phone ringing pulled me awake. I fumbled around to find it, and answered with a rather mumbled, "Hello."

"Hannah, are you alright?"

"Oh, Sam, I am now that you've called, I've been worried!"

"I know it's been a long time."

"Are you coming home soon?"

"Yes, that's why I'm calling. I have to go to Cuba and I'm wondering if you can go with me?"

"To Cuba? When?"

"In a week. I know it's very short notice, but I'll explain more when I get home."

"Oh, I can't wait to see you and I'd love to go with you!"

"I was afraid your schedule might be too full for you to be able to come."

"I'm busy for two more days, then I'll have time, and I'd make time for you no matter what."

"I'm flying into Bangor on Friday at 10:00 in the morning. I'll be on American Airlines. Can you meet me there?"

"I'll be there!"

"Is your Visa and Passport still valid?"

"Yes they are."

"I'll have the license that we'll need."

"Good, I can't wait to see you!"

"I'd like to come home by way of Greenville, maybe spend a couple of days at the camp."

"I can think of nothing better than spending two days at camp with you. I love you Sam."

"I love you too, Hannah, see you Friday."

"Bye, Sam."

All of a sudden I felt just great! It took awhile to get back to earth but I now had a really good reason to get everything done in a hurry. First things first. I needed to get that Music Quiz done.

I gathered up some song books and found my pad of paper, right where I had left it on the porch. I checked each book looking for song titles with flower names in them.

It seemed like it took me forever. My mind kept wandering back to Sam, then to Cuba, then to Greenville and Moosehead Lake. I tried to put all these things out of my mind, but it wasn't an easy task.

I finally had enough titles. I put the songbooks back where they belonged, clicked on the computer and began typing.

FLOWER SONG QUIZ

1. San Antonio _____
2. I'm Looking Over A _____
3. Second Hand_____
4. Tip-Toe Thru The _____ With Me
5. My Wild Irish _____
6. It Looks Like Rain In _____ Lane
7. The One_____That's Left In My Heart
8. When The _____ Start Blooming
9. Red _____ For A Blue Lady
10. Sweet _____
11. I Never Promised You A_____ Garden
12. Where Have All the _____ Gone?

Good Luck with this Quiz.
Everyone who participates in this Quiz will receive a Rose. The winner will receive a bottle of Champagne!

There is a trick question in this Quiz. One of these names is not a flower, but has a connection to flowers.

I printed plenty of copies, put them in a file, made a note to pick up roses Thursday morning and took a really deep breath.

I only have until bedtime to pack a bag for two days with Sam at Moosehead Lake, clean the house, wash clothes, figure out what to wear for five days at home and what to take to Cuba. I also need to do something to make me look as if I'm a sexy lady!

No problem, Hannah, just do it.

I loaded the washer, set it on Large, Permanent Press and Warm/Warm and stuffed it full of clothes. Taking a deep breath, I knew what I needed to do next was to clean the house. I hated doing housework. I mean really despised housework! Someday, when I'm a famous author, I'll have a full-time housekeeper.

Sure I will. Dream on, Hannah, but get back to work.

I began vacuuming and dusting everything as I moved through the house. I put everything

back in its proper place. I was about half done
when I stopped working and sat down. I needed
to take the time to organize my thoughts. There
was something I needed to do but I hadn't been
able to retrieve what it was.

Concentrate, Hannah, think.

Seconds later I had it! I wanted to get an
update on Pete! I called Cyrus.

"Cyrus here, how may I help you?"

"Hi Cyrus, this is Hannah. How is Pete
doing?"

"He's in detox and having a really tough
time of it. He's under constant police guard."

"Do you have the results of the mug
contents yet?"

"Not yet, but we will soon. I'll let you
know the results."

"Good, and I thought you would like to
know that Willy moved out."

"Ayah, we got the info on him from the
EMT's. You do good work, Hannah."

"Thanks, Cyrus, for all you do for others.
You've got a tough job."

"That's for sure. See you around."

I hung up the telephone and sat for awhile
just staring at nothing.

Okay, Hannah, get back to reality.

I finished the housework, cleaned the refrigerator, took out the trash and filled the dishwasher. I emptied the dryer and piled everything on the bed. I put my small suitcase nearby and as I folded clothes I either put them into the case, in the dresser or in the closet.

I straightened up and declared that all the jobs were finished and settled down on my couch. Just before I feel asleep I remembered I needed to be sure and get up real early to get ready for the next day, looking professional, not sexy - - yet.

I got up, set the alarm and went back out to the porch. The last thing I heard was an owl hooting somewhere off in the woods and my last thought before drifting off to sleep was of Sam.

Chapter Thirty-Five

Old habits are hard to lose and I was awake before the alarm went off. I grew up on a farm and I was always the first one up. I would be the only one out to the barn in the morning. I loved spending time alone talking to the animals.

I put a cup of instant coffee into the microwave and while it was heating had a shower and shampoo. I wrapped a terrycloth robe around me, took my coffee and went back to the porch to enjoy the beginning of this day.

If you have never had the opportunity to stay on a lake in Maine and be the first and only one awake, you have no idea what you have missed. It's the epitome of perfection.

Slowly, ever so stealthy, the world comes alive before your eyes and ears. Small animals make rustling noises in the bushes. Birds begin to dart from one tree branch to another, softly calling to each other. Waves begin making small slapping sounds as they come in contact with the shore. Your entire universe is coming to life. There is absolutely nothing that is comparable to beginning your day this way!

I finished my coffee and my daydreaming and began getting ready for our big day in the State Capitol. I wanted to make sure that I arrived in the parking lot at Marshwood Towers before any of the ladies did. They most likely would be nervous and I could help keep them calm.

I knew they would love eating at the Capitol's Cafeteria, and I stopped at an ATM and got cash enough to buy everyone's lunch. I pulled into the parking lot, and before I got the door open, Billy and Jimmy had arrived with the bus.

So far this morning everything was going just right, a good omen for a successful day!

Chapter Thirty-Six

Billy and Jimmy came over, opened my door and helped me exit. They were grinning like school kids who had just found out they had a day off! We walked over to the bus.

"You brought a handicapped accessible bus. How did you know we needed one? I totally forgot to tell you."

Billy shrugged and said, "Oh, we figured there might be someone who would need it."

I gave them both a hug. We stood around chatting for several minutes before the others appeared.

Miss Wood was leading the group, and Abby brought up the rear. She and her wheelchair were loaded to the hilt with the video, paper cups, bottles of water, a box of tissues and a roll of paper towels.

They were all quite somber and reminded me of school children on a field trip; they were excited but a little uneasy about what the day would be like.

We all stood and talked for a short time, and then at Miss Wood's instructions, they got back in line to board the bus. Billy got in and sat in the driver's seat and Jimmy helped each lady up the steps. When Abby's turn came, Billy lowered the handicapped ramp and Jimmy pushed Abby and her load onto it and she moved up and into the bus.

Since Miss Wood was thoroughly enjoying her role as teacher, I got on before her. She winked at me as I went past her, and took my hand for a second. Jimmy helped her climb up, then followed her and took a seat next to her. Billy shut the door and we were on our way.

At first the ladies were quiet but soon they began pointing out places they were familiar with. Soon they were laughing and having a good time. It was obvious that making the video ahead of time had been a super idea.

We got off the highway at the Augusta exit and soon the dome of the State Capitol

Building could be seen from the bus windows. It is a magnificent building and we all enjoyed the view. We reached the Capital with some time to spare. Jimmy pulled up to the side entrance and we all got off the bus. We stood around on the sidewalk until Abby joined us. A young lady met us as we entered the building.

"Good Morning, I'm Marsha, Mr. Bickford's Secretary in the Victim Advocate Office."

A chorus of hellos, and glad to meet you was returned.

Marsha explained that we would be meeting in a room that was set up for showing the video. She added that there was a restroom available close to this room. We all silently followed her down the hall to the elevators. Marsha and Miss Wood directed everyone into the two elevators.

When we got to the room, Marsha introduced us to George Bickford, the Maine State Victim Advocate. He welcomed us and thanked everyone for coming.

"Take a break if you need it. We'll begin watching the video in a few minutes." Miss Wood gave the video to Mr. Bickford and led the group back out into the hall and to the restrooms.

The ladies quietly returned and sat down. Everyone was very quiet, looking around this beautiful room and anticipating the results of their video. I always feel a sense of awe when I'm in the Capital Building and it was obvious that today I wasn't alone with this reaction.

The video began playing. It was without a doubt an extremely impressive show. When it ended there was complete stillness in the room. It seemed like it lasted forever!

Mr. Bickford was sitting with his head in his hands. When he finally looked up at us, there were tears in his eyes. He wiped his face with a handkerchief, stood up and took a deep breath. Then he looked around at our group.

"I'm practically speechless. What I just watched is almost too horrific to believe! You ladies have had to live under deplorable conditions. I am amazed that you had the strength and courage to find a way to positively prove that fraud and corruption has been perpetrated on you. You are all champions and I'm going to be a strong and proud Spokesperson for you. Before this day ends

Attorney General Mason will see this video. There will be an investigation, the problems will be fixed and the culprits will be punished. You have my word on this!"

He bent down and hugged Abby, then all the ladies gathered around him for handshakes and hugs and conversation.

I was sitting back a little from the group. It was their day and I wanted them to feel the full impact of what they had accomplished. It was reward enough for me to see the results of all their hard work.

Miss Wood started getting the ladies regrouped to go to lunch and Mr. Bickford came over and sat down beside me.

"It is my pleasure to meet you, Hannah Gray. Thank you doesn't begin to express my appreciation for what you have achieved here today."

"They did do really good, didn't they?"

"Indeed they did, super good!"

"Thank you for believing us and having us here."

Marsha came over and said, "They plan to eat at the cafeteria. I'll show them the way now, if that's okay."

"Are they paying for their own lunch, Hannah?"

"Well, no. I figured I'd treat them."

Mr. Bickford turned to Marsha and said, "Why don't you have lunch with the ladies and put all the meals on our account!"

Marsha smiled. "I was hoping you'd suggest that, we're on the way to lunch!"

She went over to Miss Wood and they all began moving out of the room.

"I have the feeling that we're going to meet again, Hannah. I'll keep you up to date on everything we do to correct this heinous situation and we will punish the bastards who perpetrated it."

"You are hero to all of these ladies, Mr. Bickford. Thank you for believing in them."

We shook hands and I left to join the others in the cafeteria.

It was fun watching everybody choose what they wanted to eat. We were pretty much scattered all over the room but I watched them mingling with others, animated by their accomplishments.

I found a spot next to Abby.

"We did good, didn't we?"

"You sure did good, Abby, and then some!"

We ate in silence for awhile.

"I got the meatballs and sauce all cooked. I'll heat it up tomorrow. Miss Wood is supervising getting the recreation room set up for lunch. She's been a great help."

"Ayah, you have all done good."

When everyone had finished eating, we made another restroom visit and returned to the waiting bus.

The ride back to Marshwood Towers was a quiet one. Many of the ladies dozed off; it had been quite a day for them, quite a week actually.

Everyone thanked Billy and Jimmy. I said "Goodbye" and "See you tomorrow" to them and all the Marshwood residents slowly returned to their rooms.

I thanked Billy and Jimmy and watched as they left for the Bus Barn.

What a day! I took all the back roads to the lake, driving really slowly. I was exhausted but feeling totally satisfied with how everything turned out.

I swam the cove and back, and then I jogged in water up to my neck until my muscles finally relaxed.

I returned to the house and opened a can of tomato soup. I poured it into my favorite soup mug, put it the microwave until it was very hot and sat in my lounge chair watching the day end.

Some days are better than others. This was one of the best!

Chapter Thirty-Seven

I was up at daylight and drove down the road apiece to a field full of daisies. I picked a huge amount of them and returned home. I left the flowers in the CRV and went in to have breakfast.

I found my old pantsuit. I would cover it with daisies. I grabbed a roll of tape and the bottle of champagne, and headed to Marshwood Towers. I wanted to get to Abby's early to help her with the food and to have time to catch her up on my schedule.

I stopped on the way and bought enough long-stemmed red roses for everyone. They all had done such a great job with the video that they deserved a rose and then some.

Abby was sitting outside in the sun watching her birds.

"Good morning, Hannah, you're here early."

"I wanted to come in time to help if I could."

"Everything's all ready, but you're in time for coffee."

She wheeled into the unit and shortly came back out; balancing a tray on her lap that had two cups of coffee sitting on it.

I hurried over and took the tray. The coffee was hot and good. We sat quietly for a time, enjoying the busy birds.

"Well, if there's nothing I can do to help, I'll catch you up on what else is happening."

"Good."

"Pete is in detox, is having a rough time of it and is being guarded all the time by the police."

"Good, the little bastard couldn't hurt enough to suit me."

"I haven't heard back from the hospital, but I bet there is fur flying around up there! They could lose their license over this."

"I still can't figure out why they didn't know how often a patent is brought in."

"Ayah, me too. The pharmacies are also going to have to do scrambling!"

"Sometimes it seems like the whole world is going downhill fast."

"Well, we've sure run into a bunch of them lately. But I'm encouraged by how yesterday turned out."

"Yes, me too."

We sipped more coffee.

"Sam called the night before last."

"He did, oh, I'm so glad! How is he?"

"He's flying into Bangor in the morning. I'm going to drive up and meet him."

"Alright, he's been gone quite awhile! I know that you've been worried."

"We're coming back here through Greenville. We'll stay there a couple of days to check out the camp."

"I'm glad you can get away from here for a spell."

"Me too. Sam will be here for the next five days and then we're going to Cuba for awhile!"

"Wow, that's great! You should have a great time."

"Ayah, I'm sure we will."

"I'll go over and check out your place. I'll call Fred if anything goes wrong."

"Thanks, Abby, you're the best friend ever."

The spaghetti sauce odor was wafting outside, and Abby went in to check on it. Miss Wood came down to help Abby. I said, "Hello" and decided to walk across the street to the house I had built there.

The new owners hadn't done much to tend all the flowers and bushes I'd planted. It really looked shabby. They had removed the garage from the middle of the house and took out the inside walls on that end of the house. What were two smaller rooms and a garage was now one huge room! They had put in a beautiful double front door. It looked great.

They had also added a two-car garage to the side of the house nearest the road.

Amazing! I couldn't get a permit to put a one-car garage there. It was too close to the road, the Code Enforcement Officer said. But now there's a two-car garage only a few feet from the same road. I guess it's not what you know but who you know that counts around here.

The flower ladies were gathering and I went back across the street. I taped all the daisies that I could to my pant suit, put my costume on, added a few daisies to my hair and joined the party.

They had all outdone themselves. We had almost every kind of flower costumes possible. There were lilies, pansies, roses, lilacs, ferns, and many more. Some were trees, one a pine and one an oak leaf. Obviously they all had enjoyed going to the flowers.

Miss Wood, Abby and a couple of others helped and soon the food was on the serving counter and everyone helped themselves. Everyone found a place at the table and things quieted down while we ate. Abby had a small bouquet of wild flowers on the table and I had put a rose by each place. This drab old recreation room had been transformed into a beautiful garden.

When everyone had finished all they could eat, we played the flower quiz game. They decided they should have a partner and when the time was up, it was no surprise when Miss Wood and her partner won. She even sang a bit of every song, to the delight of us all. She

161

was a little embarrassed to get a prize of a bottle of champagne but soon started joking about how long it would take to drink it all.

I helped on the clean-up crew, made trips to the trash container and went back to Abby's place with her.

"There's so much food left, Hannah, take some home with you."

"No way, Abby. I'm going to be gone for awhile. Freeze it up and when I get back, we'll have dinner here."

"That's a great idea."

One of the things I want to do while Sam is here is bring him over to see how they changed my old home. We'll stop in and say Hi."

"I'm so glad he's coming home. I can't imagine how hard it must be to never know where he is and what he is doing."

"Ayah, sometimes it isn't easy to love someone."

Chapter Thirty-Eight

I had crashed on the couch last night right after I set the alarm clock for 4:00 a.m. I think it had buzzed quite awhile before it finally penetrated my brain.

I stayed where I was and mentally ran through the 'To Do' list. Top of the list was to try to get me looking both demure and sexy!

Ha, Sam has been gone so long he probably won't care what I look like. I laughed at myself and went on with my list.

I needed to pack for two –possibly three days at camp and on the road.

Take the sleeping bags; we never left them at the camp.

Double check to make sure my Visa and Passport were where they should be. I sure didn't want to do that while Sam was here.

There; I was done thinking about things to do for today.

Next I decided what to wear and what to take with me and packed my suitcase. I took this and the sleeping bags out to the CRV. I checked the safe and the documents were locked up in it.

I shed my pajamas and put on my beach robe, put my biodegradable soap and shampoo in my robe pocket, and grabbed a towel. I headed for the lake.

There was just a hint in the sky that a new day was rising. There was still dew on the grass. It cooled the bottoms of my feet and worked its way up between my toes. Only a few early birds were beginning to chatter.

I swam the cove and back, quietly so not to wake up my neighbors. I had my bath and shampoo and was walking back across the lawn just as the sun fully appeared above the tree-line.

By 5:30 a.m. I was all primped and ready to go. There are really only two good ways to get from here to anywhere. I could go southeast 'til I got to the Maine Turnpike and take 95 to Bangor, or I could go north, then east and go Rt.

2 the whole way. Either way would take about the same amount of time, close to four hours.

I drive more relaxed when I'm not on the highway and I'd ridden it on the bus two days ago. The decision was an easy one for me to make; today I'd take the back roads. I backed out of my garage and went north past MickMash Mountain and continued up through The White Mountain National Forest.

There was nobody but me alive in the whole world. No, really, that's the feeling I get when I drive through this forest. Mountain peaks rise up to 3600 feet above the forests and the road winds its way through this wilderness area. I saw some wildlife, no other cars and only two people climbing one of the cliffs. By the time I reached the little town of Giliad and Rt. 2, I was totally relaxed.

I turned east to Bethel, then north and stopped in Rumford for an early take-out breakfast. I filled up my gas tank and continued east.

I was making good time and not speeding, something I tend to do on the highways. When I got to the Androscoggin River, I pulled over to the curb and sat for a few minutes looking down as its beauty.

I arrived in Farmington about the same time that all of The University of Maine, Farmington Campus faculty and students did. I had more time then any of them had and I waited while a whole bunch of them crossed the street. I glanced at my watch. Plenty of time left, but traffic no doubt would be picking up as I got closer to Bangor.

At Skowhegan I stopped at a McDonald, used their restroom, checked in their mirror to see how I was looking and got another cup of coffee. It was 8:30 and it would take about an hour more to get there.

Doing good, Hannah!

At Newport I could get onto 95 but I decided to stay on Rt. 2 and drove slowly through the little towns of Etna, Carmel and Hermon. I pulled into the airport parking lot with 20 minutes to spare.

I checked the Arrival Board. Sam's flight was on time, and I began pacing back and forth trying to walk off the remaining minutes.

I felt as if my whole body was tingling. I grinned as I remembered a time when I was a lot younger and thought that only young pups felt this way!

Chapter Thirty-Nine

I was standing a little away from the others. Sam came up the ramp and spied me immediately. We rushed at each other, silently clinging together.

"You look wonderful, Hannah, I'm so glad to be here."

"I've missed you."

"I missed you too, let's get out of here."

"Do you have any luggage?"

"No, only this carry on."

"Good."

We tightly held hands as we pushed our way through the crowd. When we got to the CRV, I passed him the keys. He opened the door and waited while I got in, then went around and got behind the wheel. Then we looked at each other and moved together. We hugged and kissed and got a little teary-eyed.

We were very quiet for awhile, just enjoying being in the same time and space. When we got out of the heavy traffic, Sam took a deep breath and turned for a second to look at me.

"Catch me up on what you've been up to."

"Lots has happened, it's a real long story."

"Long enough to get us to Greenville, I hope."

"Ayah, and then some."

"Good."

"Well, here goes, you asked for it."

I talked our way north to Dover Foxcroft, and west to Abbot Village."

"My God, Hannah, you are something else! You just never stop helping others. It's one of the many reasons I love you so much."

"I love you too, Sam."

We had reached the top of the hill overlooking Moosehead Lake and the little town of Greenville. Sam pulled onto the gravel. We unhooked our seatbelts, moved together, and sat quietly looking out over this panorama.

There is something about looking out at this fabulous view that forces you to begin to breathe deeply. Gradually we began this process and began to relax.

"It works, doesn't it?"

"It surely does! Now I know why you wanted to come up here first."

"Oh, so now along with all your other talents you can read my mind."

"I sure can, maybe we should get moving to the camp."

"I like your thinking."

We drove slowly down the hill and into the village.

"Are you hungry, we can stop for food?"

"I'm hungry all right, but not for food!"

"Now that you mentioned it, I'm not just hungry, I'm starving!"

He drove rather fast through the village, past the Lily Bay State Park and turned onto the dirt road to our camp. We made a quick stop to open the gate, parked beside the camp and began feeding each other.

Chapter Forty

It was almost dark when we felt hungry again; food hungry this time. We washed each other clean in the very cool water in our cove. A short time later, clean, dry and dressed, we drove to the The Lakeside Restaurant.

We asked for and got a table by the water and watched the full moon rise over the lake. We both ordered medium rare steaks, baked potatoes and fresh string beans. The steaks were excellent and huge. We ended up taking half the steak with us.

Dessert was fresh strawberry shortcakes. As we ate, the Katahdin headed up the Moosehead on its moonlight cruise. They had a boat full of passengers and their laughter and the boat's music soon disappeared around the bend. We left a short time later.

Down the road a piece we stopped at The Village Food Mart and bought bread, butter and coffee. Whatever we decided to do tomorrow, we'd have steak sandwiches. Back at the camp we settled into our sleeping bags, ready to get a good nights sleep.

"Do you hear from our friends, Greg and Belinda?"

"Yes, I stay in touch with some of them. The whole family is still in shock. It's tough for any of them to believe that Fred killed Victoria. It's especially difficult for Greg to believe his brother would kill anyone. It's pretty much knocked the wind out of all of them. I visit with and call Lil and Jan whenever I can but Fred's daughters have pretty much gone into seclusion."

"Jan and Lil were the ones who talked you into getting involved and then writing the book about it, weren't they?"

"Yes, at first I worried that anything I wrote in *Tainted Sand* might upset someone in the family. Then I knew that I had to write about it the best I could, and not worry about how they all would react to anything I wrote."

"It sure in hell was a tough case for you to have to deal with in many ways."

"Ayah, it brought back some haunting memories of some of the abuse cases I worked on. Do you remember the first rape case that we worked on together?"

"Do I ever! I'll never forget how you not only figured out a way to 'teach' me how to question a victim but you did it without making me look like an idiot."

"Yes, it was the first case that our Rape Council had and I just happened to be the one on duty."

"We worked a lot of cases together, and every one was a learning experience for me."

"And you taught me so much about investigating cases."

"It was really tough to be working back then on rape and child abuse cases! Nobody would believe that it was happening."

"I know. I used to say that people hated what I was doing so much that when I walked into a room, everyone would leave."

"I remember getting a phone call in the middle of that first meeting we had with the woman. I had to leave to take another case. A young man had gotten his head blown off in a drug deal gone bad. It wasn't until months later when we were in court on another case that I found out the kid was your nephew."

"I know. I'll never forget the look on your face when I told you. You stood there with your mouth open trying to associate me with that part of my family. His mother eventually died of alcoholism."

"I had heard that she did, it was really a sad situation."

"A whole lot of pain and suffering seemed to keep pulling us together."

"It sure has, Hannah, and now we are right where we were always meant to be."

We reached out to each other, held on tight and fell asleep.

Chapter Forty-One

Time really does go faster when you're having fun and our two days at camp seemed to rush right past us.

Early the next morning we brewed a thermos of coffee and made steak sandwiches. Then we got the canoe and paddles, put on our life jackets, put the cooler and coffee in the canoe and began paddling our way along the shore.

Hopefully our moose would be in the same small cove. He was there and once again raised his head up from the water to gaze at us. The weeds he was eating spilled streams of water back to the pond. He looked us over and then went back to pulling up his meal.

We paddled our way north along the shore, seeing deer and ducks. In the next cove we got a glance of a huge bear. He was eating high bush blueberries, and quickly left when we arrived.

"Want to stop and pick some?"

"You bet I would."

We paddled into the cove and beached the canoe. I took the sandwiches out of the cooler and began filling it with berries. Wild high bush blueberries were growing all around the cove. Many of the bushes were seven feet tall. The berries were big, juicy and sweet. I held the cooler while Sam sort of racked the berries into it. We retreated to the shore and sat quietly enjoying life."

"You really like picking blueberries, don't you?"

"Ayah, a long time ago, when our kids were little, we spent every weekend camping out on the back side of Frye Island in Big Sebago Lake. There was a swampy area behind our tent. It was about ten times bigger than this place. We would take 12 quart pails, tie them around our waists, and pull the berries into the pails. We all had a great time doing this together. We were the only humans on the whole north shore of the island. There were lots of bears on the island. Every time we came

176

back the bushes would be stripped clean where the bears had been feeding.

"It didn't bother you having bears close by?"

"You could see that they had been around the tent while we were gone. We had a German Shepard dog then and they never came near us with her there."

"You've always had dogs, haven't you?"

"Yes, I love all animals, especially dogs."

"It's been quite a while since Annie Love died. I figured you would have another dog by now."

"Ayah, me too. I miss having animals around me but my schedule is just too hectic now, it wouldn't be a good life for a dog. I'm on the road a lot now, speaking and selling my books. I never know where I'm going to stay at night and it's really hard to find a motel that allows animals."

"You're right, it wouldn't be fair. We better get moving and let the old bear back to his meal."

"Let's cut across the south side of Sugar Island into Beaver Cove and stop at Lily Bay

State Park. Maybe Bill and Suly will be on duty today."

Sam hugged me and grinned. "I was just thinking the same thing."

Bill and Suly were both away for the day. Bill is the Head Ranger for the Park and Suly helped run the office. Sam had known Bill since they were both State Policemen. Suly and I were part of the original group that organized REACH, the Rape Education and Counseling Helpline. We stayed in touch over the years.

We left them a note and sat on one of the lakeside benches gazing out over Moosehead Lake as we ate our sandwiches.

By the time we finished lunch the wind had shifted and was now coming out of the north. We quickly returned back to camp, glad that we were paddling with the wind. We carried the canoe and paddles back to the shed and locked the door.

Tomorrow we would clean up around the camp and make our ritualistic journey to gaze up at Mt. Katahdin and get ready to leave our refuge.

We started our last day at camp cleaning up the branches, leaves and pine needles that the wind had deposited on our yard. We made piles of the bushes and raked the leaves and needles into garbage bags. By early afternoon we began our journey east.

The old narrow, tarred-in-places road went right past our camp road and eventually led to the small settlement of Katadjo. Katadjo is on the Roach River. The Roach River begins at Spencer Bay on Moosehead Lake and empties into First Roach Pond. First Roach Pond flows into Second Roach Pond and then into Third Roach Pond. All three of these ponds are not what you'd call big. As old Mainers would say, "They are small enough to spit across."

When you get to the last pond you're in Katadjo, represented by only a dot on the map of Maine. There isn't much in Katadjo except an awesome view of Mt. Katahdin, which rises 5,268 feet into the sky! We parked the car beside the road, got out and with arms around each other stood gazing up at this majestic mountain. As we always do, we silently stood there a long time, willing this scene to stay in our minds forever!

We finally returned to camp, played a few games of Cribbage and settled down early. We were both very somber. I knew Sam was thinking about Cuba and I was getting anxious to find out why we were taking this trip.

We left our camp early the next morning. Sam had asked if I'd just as soon take the whole day on the road. He knew me so well; I loved to go for long rides.

So we went north in Greenville to Rockwood. You can't go any farther north on Moosehead Lake than the town of Rockwood. From this town north there is only a Private Road. It is open to the public but it doesn't connect with any highways. It just winds its way deep into the mountains and forests of Northwestern Maine.

No fishing from here this year. We stopped only for breakfast. We ate a huge meal of eggs, bacon, toast and coffee. Mt. Kineo cast its shadow on us, its height blocking out the sun. We finished eating and headed west.

In Jackman we turned south onto Rt. 201, the major route to Quebec. At North Forks we met up with the Kennebec River and followed it south. This entire area is as it should be, unspoiled, and pristine. Traveling through it calms your nerves and clears out all the cobwebs in your mind.

We took a detour northwest; it would take us to Rangeley Lake. By late afternoon we were at the height of land, gazing out across miles of the world as it should be.

When we entered the White Mountain National Forest the moon was shining. It cast shadows across the road that competed with our headlights. Sam turned the lights off and we slowly moved through moonlight and shadows.

"Awesome ride! Thanks."

"My pleasure!"

Chapter Forty-Two

I was awake real early and quietly got up and went to the kitchen. Sam didn't really like instant coffee, so I started real coffee brewing. I went out on the porch, covered up with my quilt and sat on the couch mentally making a 'to do' list.

First I needed to call my daughter before she left for her school. I waited until I knew she would be about ready to go and called.

"Hi, Mom, I knew it was you. Nobody else calls me this early."

"Hi Sarah. I thought I should tell you that I'm going to Cuba with Sam for a week or two."

"Great, when are you leaving?"

"The day after tomorrow."

"Is this a business or a pleasure trip?"

"Ayah!"

"I'm reading you loud and clear, Mom. Have a super vacation and call me when you can. Stay safe. I have to run, love you!"

"I love you too!"

I glanced at my watch. Richard would be on his way to the Four Seasons Café for breakfast. I dialed his cell phone number.

"What's up, Mom?"

"I'm going to Cuba with Sam the day after tomorrow for a week or two. I just wanted you to know. Abby and Fred will watch the house while I'm gone."

"I'll check it too when I'm over your way. Have a great trip, say Hi to Sam."

"Thanks, Richard, I love you!"

"Love you too, Mom!"

I made sure to always end conversations with my two great kids with "I love you." I grew up on a farm with one brother and three sisters, a puritanical Quaker mother and an overworked, underpaid Irish father. I don't ever remember hearing the word love. It was if it was embarrassing to tell someone you loved them. I guess we all took it for granted that we loved each other. But I learned how important it is to verbally tell someone you loved them.

Ok, get with it, Hannah, what's next on my list?.

Sam appeared with two mugs of coffee, passed me the one without cream and joined me on the couch.

"Please, madam, may I have part of your quilt?"

I smiled and shared the quilt. We sat quietly, enjoying the coffee.

"I think I'm next on your list, Hannah. I guess I should fill you in on the details of our trip."

He got his 'business look' on his face and began filling me in.

"I need to begin by saying that anything I tell you is confidential and cannot be repeated to anyone. You may have read about some of the things I'm going to say but much of it has not hit the tabloids yet."

We both drank some more coffee.

"We, our government, have some very serious problems at the U.S. prison camp in Guantanamo Bay in Cuba. Secret Reaction Force teams have been set up. Our interrogators in that group have initiated new and tougher physical and psychological tactics to get

184

information from the prisoners. We have been getting reports from some of the released prisoners that female civilian contractors are using abusive sexual tactics to 'break' the men into confessions of guilt."

He paused for a minute and sipped a little more coffee.

"Islamic law forbids physical contact with any women except wives or family. Some of the women interrogators involved were totally bummed out by the outrageous sexual methods they were required to use to get information from the Muslim detainees."

He looked at me, and I sort of nodded that I knew what he was talking about.

"Up until a few weeks ago we were unable to get these atrocities verified! Then we began to get information indicating that two of these women were able to make a CD ROM depicting some of these heinous interrogation methods. This is information that we must have to begin to correct this inhuman situation. Two weeks ago we learned that they had found a way to get this disk to us, but they will only deliver this disk to a woman."

"And this is where I come into the picture?"

"Yes, I got the assignment to secure the disk. The Agency felt it was extremely important to the success of this case that I go to Cuba on a Cultural License and to complete my 'cover' that my wife should go with me. I could have the choice of any of our female agents."

"But you chose me?"

"I told them I would accept the assignment under one condition. They would have to approve the only woman I would trust with my life, Hannah Gray."

"You drive a hard bargain, Sam."

"Well, they did agree and ever since I've wondered why in hell I insisted on them approving you. My decision could very well get you killed."

I put my coffee mug down, stood up and put his coffee mug down and then I sat down in his lap and looked at him, eye to eye.

"Listen carefully Sam. You and I have worked together on many cases. We took many chances and we came out on top every time. We've had something together that many people only dream of having! I would be really upset, I mean fighting mad at you, if I knew you had a choice and hadn't picked me. There is no way I would trust your life in anybody's hands but mine, either."

He started to say something and I shut him up with a kiss on his mouth, a long, sexual kiss.

He shut up, it works every time.

Later, I asked Sam for details about leaving for Cuba.

"We'll go get a rental car today and the day after tomorrow we'll drive down to Logan Airport and fly into Miami. We'll stay at The Miami International Hotel overnight. We have to be ready to leave for Cuba at four o'clock Thursday morning."

"OK, that's workable for me."

"We each need to take a suitcase but don't pack anything in it except clothes you wouldn't mind losing. We probably will be leaving in a hurry."

"What a great way to get rid of some old clothes. You've got some here that should go, too."

"Wear your money belt that goes under your clothes. Is it big enough to hold a CD ROM?"

I'll check it out. If it isn't, I'll make it bigger."

"Good."

"Do you have a carry on bag like mine?"

"Ayah."

"Ok, we'll need to put essentials in them. We have to have our credentials and anything else we don't want to lose with us when we leave Cuba."

"They should fit in front of our feet just fine no matter where we go!"

"A helicopter is going to get us out of Cuba. The details are in the works now and my contact in Cuba will keep us up to speed on the exact time and place. At certain times I'll have to leave you and get to my designated information areas."

"No wonder I haven't heard from you for quite a while."

"Have you ever flown in a helicopter?"

"Yes, I stayed over a few days in San Francisco on my way home from Japan. I flew all over San Francisco Bay and I loved it."

"How'd you get to Japan without me knowing about it?"

"It was a long time ago. I was there for four weeks."

"I've never been there; did you have a good time?"

"Yes, a very good time and a very strange time. It had something to do with the haunted house we lived in, and a little girl and a ghost. I think I'm going to include the Japan trip and the ghost story when I write *Tainted Town*."

"So, are you going to tell me about it or make me wait until I can read about it?"

"When we get back from Cuba, I'll tell you the whole story."

"Which reminds me, we're not going to come back home together."

"Oh! Why not?"

"I have to fly immediately back to Washington. I don't know how long it will take to wrap up this assignment.

"OK, I'll just fly home alone, no problem!"

"Well, they don't want you going home immediately. You're going to go to Jekyll Island for a week with a bodyguard. Then he'll fly here with you, make sure that everything's secure and then leave."

"I'm not so sure that I like that idea."

"I knew you wouldn't but it's the only way I could get them to approve you."

"OK, I guess like it or not, that's what I'll do."

"It's one of the things I don't like about this assignment. Too many others are making decisions for us."

"Do you know who the bodyguard will be?"

"Not yet."

"Ok, anything else I need to know?"

"No, we're going to have to wing some of this as we get more information!"

"Well, since you're the boss on this deal, I'll just put up and shut up."

"Good decision!"

We sat quietly for awhile, watching the waves wash over the sandy beach. It was calming for both of us to know that some things never change. Waves are forever!

"What's on the agenda for today?"

"I had planned on taking you over to show you what the people who bought my house had done to it. They obviously had a whole lot more influence on the Code Enforcement Officer than I did."

"What did they change?"

"Oh, the just took out the garage area, and made the whole end one room."

"They must have figured they didn't need a garage since they're only there summers!"

"But they do have a garage. They added a big two-car garage to the side of the house. It's only three feet from the road!"

"And that Code Enforcement jerk wouldn't let you put a one car garage there?"

I grinned at him.

"You got that right. Guess I didn't screw around with the right people!"

"Well, that's what happens when you don't play by their rules."

"Ayah! I also told Abby we would try to stop in to see her."

"We can go over."

"Let's just get the rental car this morning and hang out here 'til we have to leave."

"That sounds good to me. What's for breakfast? I'm hungry."

"Whatever you can find in the kitchen to cook will taste good to me."

"Yes, madam, I am your humble servant."

He picked up the empty mugs and headed for the kitchen.

We left a short time after we washed the dishes and returned with the rental car. On the way back we bought a few groceries to get us by the next couple of days, and we got some cash at the bank. We packed two suitcases with things we could use and lose in Cuba and loaded our back packs with essentials.

I called Abby and apologized that we wouldn't be coming over to see her.

"No problem, just enjoy and get there and back safely. Say Hi to Sam for me."

We spent what time we had left relaxing and enjoying the lake and each other.

Chapter Forty-Three

Fun and games time was over. We left for Logan Airport, and merged with all the other cars headed into Massachusetts.

"I'm glad you're driving."

Sam mumbled something nasty in reply!

At Logan we mingled with all the other Miami bound passengers, and finally got seated, buckled up and on the way. The ride was fast and bumpy. We flew through a thunderstorm somewhere over the Carolinas.

Sam asked, "Does this bother you?"

"No, I'd rather be up here in a thunderstorm than down under it. I remember playing in the woods with my sisters when there was a thunderstorm. We had to duck under three different electric fences to get back to the farm. It scared the heck out of us."

We landed at the Miami International Airport, joined the hoard at the baggage area and pushed our luggage down the long corridor toward the hotel. It was crowded, hot and noisy. As we passed a Wendy's, we just sort of looked at each other, nodded and stopped.

I travel alone a lot and it has its unique problems, like what to do with your luggage in the restrooms and walk in restaurants. I found a seat and guarded the luggage while Sam stood in line to get our food. We sat quietly eating and watching the people go by.

"I wonder what Cuban food is like?"

Sam laughed. "I was just thinking the same thing? Is that weird or what?"

We finished eating and rejoined the crowd in the corridor. We began to see signs pointing to different hotels, and soon joined new lines waiting to sign in at ours. What seemed like a long time later, we took the elevator up to the 4th floor and found Room 451.

The alarm clock woke us at 3:00 o'clock and we stumbled in and out of the shower, hurriedly dressed and headed for the Cuban Falcon Airway Terminal. We found it on Concourse E, 2nd floor, next to the Cayman

Airlines Counter. It was 4:00 a.m. and a sign indicated that our flight, #FA 621, would depart Miami at 8:00 a.m.

We looked at each other, both thinking the same thing! Four hours to get through customs.

"If we should happen to get separated Hannah, wait for me before getting in the next line. We need to stay together."

"OK, if you get held up for any reason I'll wait at the back of the next line."

"Good, I'll do the same."

We joined a long line and slowly weaved our way through Miami Customs. Security Guards were thoroughly searching everyone and their baggage. We had to remove all metal, including belts and coins, and deposit them in a plastic container. Everything in our pockets or pocketbooks was also dumped into the container. Contents of the pocketbooks were carelessly dumped out on a counter, pawed through and thrown back into it. Everyone had to take off their shoes, and they were put through a separate small x-ray machine.

Then, slowly one by one we walked under the people x-ray arbor. Both Sam and I passed this test and started to move to the next line, when the shoe x-ray machine started loudly wailing. My sneakers had flunked the test and within seconds I was surrounded by Security Guards! I had no time to even glance at Sam. Everyone was being hustled out of this area. Everyone that is, except me!

One of the Guards pushed my sneakers into my face and barked, "Yours?"

"Yes, they are."

"Give me your Visa, Passport and License, now!"

Someone had stopped the revolving turntable and all my things were still on the end of the table.

"All my belongings are still on the turntable."

Half of the guards quickly rushed over and went through everything again. They found no bombs, knives or guns, and looking extremely disappointed, they brought everything over to me.

A new demand was made to give them all of my papers!

Trying to look scared but not too scared, and willing myself to stop shaking; I found what they needed and gave my papers to one of the guards.

Then I was told to stand, legs apart and arms out straight while they ran an x-ray rod over my whole body!

They looked rather disappointed that no alarms went off.

I watched as six of the guards paraded down the hall with my paperwork and my sneakers. The remaining guards escorted me into an empty room and sort of plunked me into a chair.

My guards left the room and slammed the door shut. I heard the door lock click into place!

I sat there, holding my knapsack very close to my chest, sort of like protection. I wanted to yell and I wanted to cry! I willed myself to take deep breaths and gradually settled down. I figured that I was being monitored and I very much needed to look calm cool and collected.

Then I got mad! How in hell could this have happened? How come my sneakers set the alarm off? What did they think I had in them, a knife? Someone a few months ago had tried to get into America with a knife in their shoe! Ayah that must be it. I look so damn much like a terrorist!

I sat there silently saying all the old Maine swear words I knew. I could see the headlines in all the newspapers. Homeland Security saves hundreds from another terrorist!

My next thought was, *"Oh, my God, this will totally destroy this trip for Sam."*

I tried to keep my 'I'm not worried look' and I sat very still. It seemed like hours but in reality was only twenty minute, before I heard the lock turn and one guard, holding a clipboard, came into the room. He handed me my sneakers, Passport, Visa and License. He sullenly waited while I put on my sneakers and put my paperwork back where it belonged. I glanced at his clipboard. There was a single sheet of paper on it. It was covered with scribbled words.

He had an extremely disappointed look on his face as he escorted me to the end of the line of people waiting to get to Cuba.

Sam was the last person in line. He said nothing, just took my hand and led me the rest of the way to the airplane. Somewhere along the way another group of guards was asking everyone how much cash we were taking to Cuba. When my turn came I answered, $800.00 and feared that I would be taken out of line again. Not quite paranoia, but close. We were waved on and with Sam almost walking on the backs of my sneakers; we found our seats, put our knapsacks in front of our feet, and buckled up.

I whispered, "I'm so sorry, Sam, this could have ruined our trip."

"It's okay, Hannah, everything is alright, I love you. Now take some deep breaths and don't worry. You did just great!"

I took his advice. As I calmed down I became aware of something happening to my feet. They were beginning to feel very hot, as if I was standing on a hot stove! Maybe I had walked through something I shouldn't have when I didn't have my sneakers on. I'd try ignoring this also. Something else I couldn't fix, so just try to forget it.

Twenty minutes later we were walking across the steamy tarmac in Cuba. We were herded into a large room and for the next seven hours we stood in lines waiting to get through

Cuban customs. We were packed into this space that, big as it was, wasn't large enough to hold all of us. There was no ventilation in the room and it soon got much to warm to be comfortable.

Occasionally someone would enter or leave the room and a draft of fresh air would make us believe that you could indeed live to get out of here and to our hotel! The longer we had to stand in line, the more my feet hurt. The pain was beginning to be extremely uncomfortable. I didn't want to complain, but they were beginning to feel as if they were on fire! Sam was just great. He knew I must be hurting, and he kept a conversation going.

We crept closer to the front of our line and finally it was our turn to go through customs. I passed my I.D. things through the slot in the window and stood stoically while the agent looked first at me, then at my passport photo a number of times! He finally decided I was me and handed everything back through the hole.

He nodded and in perfect English said, "Enjoy your time in Cuba."

I replied, "Thank you."

Sam followed me through the line, and we dragged our luggage to the waiting buses. We were sort of herded into the buses, twelve people to each bus. The guide was a young Cuban man who spoke excellent English. He explained that we would all stay together on this same bus, Number Ten, for the whole week and that he would be our guide the entire time.

"We won't be able to check into our hotel rooms until later. We will tour part of Havana and go to lunch at the Tocoror Restaurant." He passed bottles of water to the front seat people, who in turn passed them along to all of us. "You will get a bottle of good water each day. Do not drink water here unless it is in a sealed bottle."

My feet were really extremely painful and I dug through my knapsack, found my Advil and washed two of them down with the water.

"Ok, Hannah?"

"I should have taken these sooner, I'll be alright, thanks."

The short drive through Havana ended at the Tocororo Restaurant and we were seated at tables for six in an outside dining area. We were all served the same, excellent lunch and musicians sang as they roamed in and around us. I love music and relaxed a little as the Advil and food took my mind off my burning feet.

Two hours later, when we finally got a room at the Presidente Hotel, the pain had returned and my feet hurt so much that I was hobbling! Sam helped me to a chair. I put my head back and tried not to cry as he began taking off my sneakers.

Sam's "Oh, my God!" got my attention and I looked down at my feet. Brown liquid 'stuff' was oozing up around my toes and my nylons were dripping with goop! Sam carefully began getting the nylons separated from my feet. The bottoms and a half inch up the sides of my feet were a reddish brown color!

Sam checked my sneakers. The inside of them were coated with this disgusting chemical! When he tipped them upside side, the stuff began running onto the floor.

"Sit still Hannah, while I put these in the bathroom sink and get some cold water into the tub. We need to get your feet soaking in a hurry!"

He was back in a flash with wet towels and laid them out on the floor, making a path to the tub. Then he carefully helped me walk to the tub. I sat on the edge with my feet immersed in water and watched as the brown gook gradually dissipated into the water.

Sam emptied the water, rinsed out the tub and added new water. We went through this procedure a dozen times. Then Sam soaked a washcloth, added soap and very, very carefully washed my feet.

"Did you bring other shoes with you?"

"No, only a pair of sheepskin lined leather slippers."

"They will have to do; you sure as hell can't wear these sneakers ever again! I'd like to take them back with us and have them tested, but I guess that won't be practical. I'll wrap your nylons up in something and have them tested instead."

"Did you bring any salve with you?"

"No, but there's a bottle of hand lotion with aloe, maybe that would help."

Sam got the lotion. Then he carefully dried each foot and gently covered them with the lotion.

"How bad are they?"

"Well, they're dyed a deep shade of reddish brown all over the bottoms of both feet and for about a half inch up all around, including between your toes! There are no places where the skin has been abraded so hopefully the lotion will help ease the pain."

"If you're alright sitting her for a little while, I'll go down and see if I can get an ice bag, it would maybe stop some of the pain."

I tried to smile. "I'll be fine, Sam. Wow, what a great start to our 'vacation'."

"One thing I have always known is that life with you is never dull or boring, Hannah. It's one of the many reasons that I love you."

A quick kiss and he left to find some ice.

Sam was soon back with the ice and helped me walk to the bed. He put the ice bags on my feet and covered me up.

"I have to be somewhere at a certain time, Hannah. I need to go now. Are you sure you're ok here alone?"

"I won't be if you let me get in the way of what you have to do, Sam. Go, but if you can, will you bring some bottled water or soda and maybe something to snack on back with you? I don't think I want to go out to dinner tonight."

"Will do; try to get some sleep, Hannah."

I guess I slept! I woke up to darkness when I heard the door opening.

"It's just me, Hannah."

"I'm glad your back."

Sam got me two more Advil. I drank a lot of water, ate some chips and laid back down while he put more lotion on my feet.

"They're really feeling much better, Sam. I should be fine by morning. How did everything go?"

"Everything's on schedule."

"Good!"

"Yes, it's important that we stay on schedule from now on. I'm confident that this will all go smoothly."

"That's encouraging. Now how about helping me stay warm for the rest of the night?"

"I'll be glad to; I'm really good at that."

"Ayah!"

Chapter Forty-Four

By morning my feet were feeling much better. Our itinerary was a morning bus tour of Modern Havana. We would have lunch at a restaurant called La Celilia. In the afternoon we would have a bus trip to the sulphourous and healing waters of the San Juan River.

I laughed, "They must have known I would need to soak my feet today."

We showered and got ready for the day. Sam tended to my feet again, making sure there were still no open wounds.

I could get really used to this time of treatment."

"Anything for the lady I love."

"Talk like that will get you anything you want."

"It better or I'll quit this job."

Sam very carefully helped me put on a pair of cotton socks and I slid my feet into my slippers.

"OK?"

I smiled, "OK."

"You'll need to dry your feet off after you soak them in the river." He put a towel in my backpack.

We went downstairs, joining the others for a breakfast buffet. There were only a few seats left and we heard someone call, "There are two seats left here, I'll save them for you."

"Why don't you sit there now? I'll get breakfast for both of us."

I went over and took one of the empty seats. The lady who had called to us said, "Welcome, I'm Della Howe. She was a beautiful lady and she introduced the others at the table. They were all Black Americans and two of them were sisters. One of them was a man, Thomas, a retired teacher. They were having a great time, and it was contagious.

Between all of us, we represented six different states. We made sure that we all sat together for the rest of the week.

Breakfast at the Presidente Cafeteria was an amazing event. The room was exquisite with an enormous amount of food and beverages that lined one entire wall. A combo was playing at one end of the room. Sam came with our breakfast and immediately Thomas began a discussion about education and politics with him.

The bus trip around Havana showed us the best and the worst of the city. We were really impressed that our guide openly spoke of what was happening in Cuba.

"I was born in Cuba. I'm 42 years old. I am an only child and live with my mother and father. Sometimes my girlfriend lives with us and sometimes we stay where there is more privacy." We clapped. He smiled.

"I graduated from the University with a degree in English and Literature. In Cuba all education is free but you have to get top grades on the entrance test to get into the degree program you want. I give one third of what I make as a Guide to the people who set these tours up, one third to the government and one third to my parents. My father is unable to work."

We stopped for lunch at Tocororo Restaurant again, then continued on to the San Juan River.

Sam walked down the winding stairway to the river with me and sat on a large rock while I soaked my feed in the cold, healing waters of the river.

"You should be soaking your feet too, Sam."

"Probably should soak my whole body."

"Probably would scare everybody back to the bus."

"Everyone but you, that would be great. We could heal our entire bodies."

The bus driver started blowing the bus horn, his signal that we needed to move on. We all climbed back up the stairs, took one more look down at the San Juan River and went on to the rest of the day.

Dinner was at the Don Cangry Restaurant. We were seated right next to the live combo. As we settled into our places, the bank started playing 'Autumn Leaves', a favorite of mine. I was tapping my fingers and feet, and singing along, thoroughly enjoying their music. I felt a hand on my shoulder, looked up and the leader was handing the mike to me, motioning me to join them!

I looked at Sam; and he smiled which I took to mean 'no problem' so I joined the band. They played 'my song' again. This time I got everyone at our table and then the entire group singing. The band members were really enjoying themselves and everyone was laughing and clapping and having a great time.

The band leader thanked me. I thanked him and gave him a big hug. Everyone clapped again. The evening evolved into one of the best times ever for us.

Back at the hotel, I realized that I hadn't thought about my hurting feet for hours.

"Could it be possible, Sam, that the San Juan River was really healing water?"

"With you I really believe anything is possible."

"Ah, you say the nicest things."

"I know."

"We're scheduled to enjoy a walking tour of Old Havana tomorrow. If my feet still hurt in the morning, I don't think I'd really enjoy it! I can just hang out here, or if I can find a place to buy a disk about Cuba before the Revolution, I could take a taxi to buy it. I have three speaking engagements about Cuba all set up back home and I could use some extra information."

"I heard Della saying she wasn't too keen about this walk. Maybe you could get her to hang out with you."

"That a great idea."

"You can talk to her at breakfast."

"You sure you don't mind walking it without me?"

"I have to take a detour part way through the walk so I couldn't be with you for the whole time anyway."

"Then, it's settled, I'll spend a day taking good care of my feet."

"I want to check your feet again to make sure there are no open sores."

I dutifully laid down on the bed so he could check them.

He checked my feet and pronounced them healing just fine. Then he checked some other parts of me to see how they were doing. Everything seemed to be working perfectly!

Chapter Forty-Five

We were on the end of the breakfast line, again.

"If you find us a table, I'll get the food."

"Sounds good, only just coffee and something sweet for me"

I could see that there was three places left at the table with our new friends, and I weaved my way through the crowd to join them.

"Where's Della, I hope she's not ill?"

Thomas said that she's just tired and was going to sleep in, then just hang out here.

"I'm going to stay here too; maybe we can hang out together."

Sam arrived with our food and very shortly everyone was herded onto the buses.

I was almost alone in the cafeteria. One of the waiters came over to ask if I wanted anything.

"Another cup of black coffee would be nice, thank you."

He brought the coffee and I asked him if he knew where I could buy a CD ROM about Cuba after the Revolution and in English.

"I'm sorry, I am not aware of where you could obtain this, but I'll ask around in the kitchen."

I thanked him and sat sipping my coffee and enjoying the music.

"Well, good morning, did you miss the bus?"

"Good morning, Della. No, I wasn't up to taking a long walk."

"Neither am I, let me get some food and I'll join you."

A short time later, the waiter returned and gave me a piece of paper with a name and address on it.

"Go to the Centro De Prensa International at Calle 23 No. 152 esq. a O., Vedada, Plaza. They should have what you want there. It's quite far, I'll call an el taxi for you if you so wish."

"Thank you, that would be good," and I passed him a $5.00 bill.

"Gracias madam, it has been my pleasure."

"Want some company? I'd love to tag along with you?"

"I'd love to have you come with me."

We finished our breakfast, made a quick stop in the lady's servicios, and went out on the porch to wait for the el taxi!

The cabbie was a young, nice looking Cuban lady! She jumped out and opened the door for us, asked where we wanted to go, and wound her way downtown through the heavy traffic. She stopped in front of the Centro De Prensa International building and held the door while we got out.

"We shouldn't be very long; will you please wait here for us?"

"Si, Senora."

We immediately ran into a problem. Nobody in the busy lobby could speak English and neither Della nor I could speak enough Spanish to make our needs known. We were standing there wondering what to do next when a tall, well-dressed man came up to us.

"I am Amilel Attarre Tilhdut, a Correspondent for Percodico Opcion Ecuador.

Is there something I can do to help you, madam?"

He handed me his business card.

"I'm an author and speaker in the United States and I am trying to find a CD ROM of life in Cuba after the Revolution, and it has to be in English. I was told I might be able to buy one here."

"Let me speak for you. This may take a little time. Do have an el taxi waiting for you?"

"Yes we do."

"I'll make sure they wait for you."

"Thank you so much."

We sat on one of the benches and waited while he dashed outside, came back in and went into one of the rooms across from us.

Della and I sat watching the people around us.

"Some of these people don't seem too happy to be here."

"I noticed the same thing!"

I was getting a little fidgety when our interpreter came over to us.

"They have what you require but have to order it. I took the liberty of doing so. It will be ready the day after tomorrow."

"Thank you so much, I really appreciate it! I'm glad you were here to help us."

"I've just finished covering the International Film Festival at the Hotel Nacional. I have a rent close by and I stop in here often. I believe that the Hotel would have what you require. It would be my pleasure to walk with you to there."

I looked at Della, she looked at me and we both sort of agreed.

"Thank you, it would be good to get what I need today."

He escorted us outside, went over and told the taxi driver to wait, took my arm and with Della following we headed up the narrow sidewalk to the Hotel Nacional.

A short time later, we crossed the street to this magnificent hotel! He was greeted with hugs and kisses by many of the actresses still milling around in the hotels huge outside veranda.

Della and I both relaxed for the first time since he introduced himself, it was plain that he was who he said he was! We stood watching him go from one vender's booth to another.

"I apologize. It is a wrong time to be trying to obtain what you need. Business here for all of them has been excellent and they are out of many things, including what you wish to have."

"I really appreciate all that you have done to help me. I am just glad that I could have the chance to see this magnificent hotel."

He reached out, took my hand and held it all the way back down the hill to the taxi.

I had the feeling that Della was probably getting a real kick out of this.

The taxi was waiting for us. My new friend paid her, helped Della into the el taxi and than kissed me on the cheek, winked at me, and helped me into the el taxi and left.

Della and I looked at each other and burst out laughing.

"What fun! There is never a dull moment when I'm hanging out with you!"

"Ayah!"

Chapter Forty-Six

"How did your day go, Sam?"

"It was very interesting. We walked through Old Havana's narrow streets. There are no sidewalks and no cars. The houses all are built to the edges of the streets. Most of them had their doors and windows open and were selling handmade items. The buildings are badly in need of repair. It was a long, hot walk."

"I'm glad I didn't go."

"We did have a chance to stop when we got to the San Francisco Square. There were little café tables and chairs all around the square. This area was entirely under water until they filled it in and built warehouses, cantinas and restaurants. We could take a horse and buggy ride if we wanted to. I just sat and watched everything that was going on. There were children playing ball, some beggars, two policemen who just stood in one spot and never spoke to anyone, and there was a good looking prostitute who had on a beautiful full-length pink lace dress with nothing on under it."

"I can tell that you didn't miss a thing!"

"Nary a thing. I knew you would want to hear about every detail."

"Ayah, what's on tap for tomorrow?"

"We're supposed to go up into the mountains west of Havana and visit a school but I need to be available here."

"I'm really interested in what their schools are like, but that probably wouldn't be much fun for you anyway."

"Don't wake me up when you leave."

I didn't and hurried down to breakfast. Della was entertaining the group with stories of what happened yesterday.

"This lady isn't safe to be traveling alone; I'm just going to have to go back with her when she picks up the CD ROM."

The trip up into the mountains was a long ride but well worth it! We stopped in one spot where you could look out at the Caribbean Sea in one direction and turn around and see the Gulf of Mexico in the other.

The school was high up in the mountain, a one-story, well maintained K thru Six school. We arrived just in time for lunch and all went to different classrooms to eat with the students. Lunch was black beans, bread and water. The teachers translated all of our questions to the students and they smiled at us and answered them. There were about fifteen students to a room. Each room had a blackboard, a TV and two long tables with benches along each side. The teacher had a small desk sort of tucked into a front corner.

After lunch the students took all of the lunch trays away and stayed outside to play. When we all gathered to watch them, they hurriedly got into lines to have their pictures taken! They were all dressed in uniforms, and obviously were contented and happy.

When we got back to the hotel, Sam was gone. I left him a note, met Della in the lobby, called a taxi and went back to the Centro DePrensa International building to pick up my CD.

I showed one of the young ladies the Ecuadorian Correspondent's business card and she motioned for us to sit in some chairs that were sort of in a semi-circle, off to one side of the room.

I have always been a people watcher and today was no exception. Across the room a young man was sitting between two older men. They were obviously questioning him and he was not enjoying himself at all! My antenna went up immediately! I got a prickly feeling between my shoulder blades that I get whenever something didn't seem right. I knew from past experiences to pay attention to this feeling.

I motioned to Della. We stood up and I smiled at a couple of women who had been standing nearby. I said, "We have to leave now, thank you." We headed for the door.

They moved into our path, smiled and held up two fingers and in English said, "Wait two minutes!"

We sat back down. I sat there damning myself for getting into yet another mess. *If I get out of here without fouling up Sam's week, it'll be a wonder*!

We once again stood up and just sort of meandered around the room, looking at pictures on the wall, admiring a piece of furniture, smiling at each other and at other people, working our way closer to the exit!

This time one of the women said, "This way ladies, and she led us toward an open door. I was working at looking like this was just an everyday occurrence for me when a well-dressed gentleman stepped out the door.

"Let me try to help you. Come in please."

We stepped inside. I shook his outstretched hand and said, "Thank you." I quickly explained why I was there.

He handed me his business card and said, "I am Riol Rial Pirog. How did you get Amidal's business card?"

"He offered to help me because I don't speak any Spanish!"

I handed him my business card.

"So, you are not a foreign correspondent?"

"No, I'm an author, a publisher and public speaker and I only wanted a CD ROM in English to have first hand information from

Cubans about what life is like after the Revolution."

"Then you are not here on a Correspondent's license?"

"No, I'm here on a Cultural license."

"I'm really sorry, Ms. Gray, but we can't sell to you because you have the wrong license."

I started backing up towards the door and Della was not far behind.

"I'm so sorry to have taken so much of your time; I didn't understand. I really appreciate your taking time to talk with me."

"Wait, please, I may be able to help you!"

He left and Della and I stood there, saying nothing. I kept looking at his business card that almost seemed to be glued to my hand, trying to comprehend what this place really was.

A few minutes later he returned. He had a CD ROM which he passed to me. In a very loud voice he said, "This is in both Spanish and English. It's title is 'La utopia realizada, the attained Utopia'! I cannot sell you this, I LOAN it to you. You know what LOAN means?"

"Yes, I get the information that I need from this and return it to you."

"Yes, it is only a LOAN."

223

By this time my brain was telling me that I was dealing with a Cuban Government Agency and we were being taped and probably videoed! I concentrated hard on just looking at him.

"Right, I send it back to you at this address." I ran my finger across the mailing address on his business card.

"Good, you mail it back to me at this address." He picked up my finger and ran it across his e-mail address!

"You understand this is only a LOAN?"

"Yes, I understand. Thank you very much for the LOAN of this. I'm sure it will help me tell people the real story of Cuba!"

As I turned to leave he moved closer, hugged me and whispered, "You are a neat lady, thank you!"

Debby and I did a good job of acting nonchalant as we worked our way out of the lobby, down the steps and to one of the el taxi's that was waiting nearby. The cabby jumped out, opened the door and we sank into the back seat.

"Holly shit, Hannah! What a performance!"

"Probably it was one of my best, Della!"

"We were being watched, weren't we?"

"No doubt about it! It's not something I want Sam to hear about; I think he would be very upset at me!"

"I won't say a word, nobody would believe me anyway."

Sam wasn't there when I got to our room. I wrapped the CD ROM up in some underwear and tucked it down to the bottom of my knapsack. Then I put the small plastic bag of laundry on top of it. There was absolutely no way that I could ever let Sam know how this day had gone. Well, maybe when we were old and gray and needed a good laugh!

Sam arrived and asked how my day went. I talked about the school, the students and the teacher!

"How did your day go?"

"Everything is still on schedule. When we leave here tomorrow for the City of Trinidad, we won't be coming back here."

We both flopped onto the bed. I dozed off and woke when Sam said, "Hannah, wake up, we have a lot to do before tomorrow."

We began getting everything that we would need into our backpacks. We would have to take the suitcases with us tomorrow, but they would be left in our hotel room in Trinidad.

Neither one of us had eaten dinner. We went downstairs but the dining room was closed. We went into the bar and had beer, pretzels and chips for our last meal in Havana.

Chapter Forty-Seven

The trip to Trinidad seemed to go on forever. We went west through farm country to Santa Clara. Along the way we passed tobacco and sugar cane fields. Peons with machetes were cutting the grass and crops beside the road. Others were loading the crops onto old wooden wagons, with wooden wheels. The wagons were hitched up to oxen.

When we got to Santa Clara, our guide explained that we would be honored by having a police escort through the city. Sam leaned close and said, "I wonder what's here that they don't want us to see."

We left Santa Clara and headed south. There was still a long way to go to get to Trinidad. Somewhere along the way some of the group began asking how far it was to the next restroom! A short time later, the bus driver pulled over in front of a small house. He hurried from the bus and hugged the woman who had just come out of the house! The guide explained that this was the driver's house and anyone who needed to could use their bathroom. Those that took advantage of this opportunity left money for the family. This obviously was a planned stop to give the driver a chance to make a few extra dollars.

We finally arrived at our hotel. It was on a long, sandy peninsula that jutted out into the Caribbean. Sam and I checked out the dining area, located the kitchen down a long hall and found that the restrooms were on the way to the kitchen! Then we went upstairs to our room.

The room was hot and stuffy. We opened one of the windows on the ocean side and wonderful fresh air rushed in.

"It's sort of calling for us go outside."

"That's exactly what I was thinking."

We rummaged around in our suitcases and changed into old shorts and tee shirts. I grabbed two towels from the bathroom and we went downstairs to the lobby.

There were vendors everywhere and most of them spoke English. We passed by a vendor selling tee-shirts. "Tee shirts, only 5 American dollar!" We couldn't resist and bought two of them that had Cuba printed on them. "Gracias, Americans nice."

We left the lobby, crossed the street, took off our sneakers and walked barefoot through the beautiful white sand. We stopped only to put our sneakers and towels on lounge chairs and soon were swimming in the Caribbean Sea.

We spent the evening walking the beach looking for seashells, swimming and sitting in the lounge chairs. Everyone else was in the dining room. We could hear the talking, the laughter and the music but it all just seemed to be far away from where we were.

We heard someone coming across the sand and a few minutes later our Guide sat down on the sand beside us.

"Is it alright if I interrupt your solitude?"

"You certainly can."

We listened as this young man told us about his life in Cuba.

"I was born after The Revolution and my life is much better than my parents had. Before the Revolution only the rich could own property and do anything they wanted to. Everyone else had nothing."

"Now we can buy a home. We only have to find one we want to buy, fill out papers and give them to the Government. We pay them every month and when we've paid the entire amount we get a deed to our home. There is no interest added onto the cost and once it is ours we can sell it if we want to."

We asked him many questions and then he asked us many questions about what life was like in America.

"I think I have taken a longer break that I should have. I've enjoyed our discussion. Thank you, I'll see you tomorrow."

The moon was now shinning brightly, the waves were calm and the whole world seemed to be beckoning for us to go swimming again.

It was almost midnight when we returned to the real world.

Chapter Forty-Eight

Morning came quickly and we crowded back onto the buses. The driver did a wonderful job of maneuvering the bus through the small, narrow streets of downtown Trinidad and pulled off the road a short distance from the Infirmary that we were going to visit.

A lady dressed in a white uniform met us at the door. Our Guide introduced us to Dr. Darti. She was obviously pregnant, and she looked uncomfortable as she stood while we all tried to crowd into one of the two small rooms that was her clinic. She answered all of our questions and our guide translated them for her and us.

She was eight months pregnant with her third child. She lived just across the tiny patio area with her family.

The clinic served 800 families. If they couldn't walk to the clinic, she walked to their homes.

She was an employee of the government and they supplied her with all medicines and equipment

Yes, she did operations in the other room.

If she had a wish list, she would ask for antibiotics.

Yes, the government paid her! The amount, the equivalent of $20.00 American dollars a month.

Yes, the government paid for her apartment.

Yes, the government paid for all of her college expenses.

The questions went on and on and the line of people waiting outside to see the doctor was getting very long. We thanked her and got back on the bus,

We had not been so quiet on the whole trip as we all were now!

I guess we were probably all thinking the same thing. The two little rooms were not as clean and well stocked as a school nurse's room back home.

The bus took us as far as it could. The streets were too narrow for a vehicle and we all walked around the town of Trinidad. The streets were paved with all shapes and sizes of rocks making it extremely difficult to walk on them. When there was a sidewalk it was narrow and badly in need of repair. The only ones who seemed to be enjoying the streets were cowboys on horses. They galloped full tilt down the roads, stopping only to jump off and pick up any money the tourists threw to them.

There were also wall to wall venders everywhere. The streets were full of people selling everything from beautiful lace items to musical instruments and junk. It was sometimes almost impossible to get through the crowd.

We were all supposed to meet for lunch. We pushed our way through the maze to The LaBona Restaurant.

We were ushered to tables out on the back patio. The restrooms were directly to the left of this area and there was no wall between where we ate our food and the toilets. You could see people's feet at the bottom and when they were standing you looked them in their eyes, or at the back of a man's head. There also were no screens anywhere and the flies were having a feast.

Complaints were made and a large group of us asked to be bused back to the hotel. We spent the rest of the afternoon making up for getting very little sleep the night before. We set the alarm clock. We had much to do before this day ended, and we couldn't take a chance on sleeping too long.

"We need to sit as close to the kitchen as we can! Our contact is one of the waitresses."

He reached into his backpack and took out a small round object. He handed it to me.

"Put this in your pant's pocket. It has a buzzer in it and when you feel the buzzer going off, go immediately to the lady's room. The waitress will follow you in and give you a CD ROM! Go into one of the stalls and put it into the waist wallet under your clothes. Then quickly leave the restroom! OK so far?"

I nodded that I was ok.

"I won't be far behind you. I'll follow you as far as the men's room, and will be in the hall when you come out. We'll follow the waitress out through the kitchen to the utility door and cut across the sand towards the sea. A helicopter will pick us up and fly us out of here!"

Sam paused for a few minutes, and then continued.

"If anything goes wrong - if something should happen to me - you have the information and you must keep going and get out of the area! If there had been any way to have this passed directly to me I wouldn't have involved you in this!"

"I'm ok with this, Sam, I really am. We're going to get out of here together."

We left the room clean and neat. The only trace to us would be the suitcases, and there was nothing in them to identify us. We went down to the lobby and mingled with the others in the group, chatting and laughing as if we were your average tourists.

We did make sure, however, that we were the first in line for dinner and sat at the table closest to the kitchen.

I quietly told Sam that I wanted to check out the facilities while I had a chance to. The booths were the typical Cuban restaurants ones, swinging doors with a foot of open space at the bottom and when you stood up you could look out over the top of the door.

The music was very loud so it was almost impossible to talk to each other. The waitresses had just served us fresh fruit cups when I felt my buzzer vibrating. I gave Sam a nudge and headed for the bathrooms!

A waitress followed me into the lady's room. She handed me a paper bag. I noticed that someone was in the first stall so I quickly went into the next one. I had just shut the door when I heard the waitress yell, "Sir, you can't go in there!" Then she screamed in pain! I quickly stepped up onto the seat and slouched down.

A shot rang out and the lady in the first stall screamed! I heard a thud and looked down and saw blood coming under the partition!

I was frantically trying to get the disk hidden when I heard Sam yell at the man. There was the sound of someone else hitting the floor. Then someone came into the bathroom.

"Oh, my God, I've killed Hannah! Damn it all to hell; I never should have involved her in this. Oh, Hannah, what am I going to do without you?"

I stood up on the seat and looked down at Sam. He was kneeling down with his head in his hands and tears were dripping through his fingers.

"Oh, thank God it's you Sam; I thought the guy had killed you and whoever is in the first stall and was coming after me!"

Sam straightened up with jerk and looked in disbelief at me. He turned pale and I thought he might faint!

"Hannah, I thought you were killed!"

"If there hadn't been someone in the first stall, I would have been. That poor lady got whacked instead!"

I stepped down off the toilet seat, fumbled around to get the door open and rushed into Sam's arms. It only took us a few seconds to realize that we both were alive!

"Let's get out of here and finish this project."

The waitress was alive but not in very good shape. We stopped by her for only a second and Sam bent down to tell her that she had done a great job.

We ran to and through the kitchen and out into the darkness of a moonless night. We could hear the thumping noise of the helicopter. We ran full tilt down across the sand and got to the water's edge. The helicopter hovered over us. The door opened and the rope ladder was dropped down. We both jumped onto it and we were headed out to sea before we were pulled inside!

We were led to some seats. Sam seemed in a daze!

"Do you want the CD ROM now?"

He sort of jerked back into reality.

"Yes, Hannah, thank you for getting me back on track."

I reached under my panties, unhooked the clasp, pulled the waist wallet out and put it on his lap.

"I thought you had been killed!"

"I know!"

"Where were you, I didn't see anyone else but the dead person in the john?"

"I jumped up onto the seat and crouched down when I heard a commotion."

"I will never forgive myself for getting you involved in this!"

"Oh, for heavens sake, would you stop with that crap? I'm not a child! I could have refused, you know. But I didn't, and we're both alive!"

"You could be dead and I would have caused it to happen!"

"Snap out of it, Sam! I thought you had been killed too and I know what a shock it was to have me suddenly appear over the door but you still have to finish your part of the job. We did good; you and me together."

Sam took a deep breath, leaned back in his seat and stopped talking. I leaned over, gave him a long, long kiss and we clung together until we both were back to normal.

Chapter Forty-Nine

We set down at the end of a long runway at the Miami International Airport close to a U.S. Air Force Jet.

"I'll be right back," Sam said.

I watched out the window as he ran over to the Jet. A few minutes later Sam and another man were running back to the helicopter.

"Hannah, this is Bob Abel. He is going with you to Jacksonville Airport. Then he will drive you to Jekyll Island for a week or two. From there you both will fly into Pease Air Force Base in New Hampshire and he will drive you home."

"You don't have to go to all this bother, Sam. I don't need a bodyguard and I really just want to go home."

"It's important for me to know that you are not being followed and that you're safe,

Hannah. Bob will make sure that you stay safe."

"You know best."

"I have to leave right now."

He put his hand on my shoulder, gave me a quick peck on my cheek and ran back to the waiting jet.

I watched him climb up into the plane as we lifted off the runway heading for Jacksonville.

My babysitter quickly sat down next to me and buckled up. He turned to me and smiled.

"Hi, my name is Robert Uto Abel; my friends call me Bob. You wouldn't believe how much I get ribbed with a moniker like R. U. Able."

He laughed with pleasure at his memories, I guess. I really didn't think he was that funny and when I didn't laugh with him he abruptly stopped. He looked at me all of a sudden with a serious expression.

"I know you don't think you need me around but I have a job to do and I'm damn good at it. For the next few weeks we are Mr. and Mrs. Jim Peters. Sally and Jim on a vacation in the South. We have a real need to act as if we liked each other. Do you think that you are able to play your part?"

He burst out laughing again and repeated, "I'm able are you able?"

His laughter was contagious and I began to calm down a little. My nerves were still strung up tight and my feet were really hurting. I was also upset with myself for questioning Sam's judgment.

I leaned back in the seat and tried to shut out the noise of the helicopter and think of nothing, my favorite way of relaxing.

Bob was looking out the window on the other side of the helicopter and I turned to look at him. I figured I should memorize what he looks like just in case. He sure didn't look like a bodyguard. He was skinny and maybe a couple of inches taller than me. His hair, what there was left of it, was a yellowish gray color. He had a rather thin face and wore glasses that appeared to be too big for his face. In the short time I looked him over; he pushed them up off the end of his nose four times. He really looked quite puny, not at all like someone I would have hired to be my bodyguard!

Without turning to look at me he said, "I hope you like what you see." Then he turned to me and began laughing again.

We set down at the Jacksonville Airport right next to a car that was waiting at the end of one of the runways. Robert, ah, Jim got out, spoke with the driver a minute, then they both came back on the helicopter. The driver sat down, buckled up and we (known as Jim and Sally Peters) left the helicopter. It lifted off and was out of sight before we got to the car.

Jim opened the car door and I slid onto the seat. Jim reached for the seat belt, leaned across me and hooked the seatbelt, pausing as he brushed across my breasts.

Grinning at me he said, "You need to remember to buckle up, always."

I reached behind him and gave him a karate chop behind his left knee!

He yelled, jerked upright and hit the back of his head on the door frame. He took a few steps backwards, holding his head with one hand and his leg with the other.

He hobbled around the car, got in and buckled up. Then he turned to me and said, "What in hell did you do that for?"

"Let's get something settled right now. I don't need you to protect me. I don't want you protecting me and if you touch any part of my body again you'll find out how much more I know about protecting myself. Do I make myself clear?"

"Perfectly clear, Mrs. Peters, I hear you loud and clear."

I was exhausted! I closed my eyes but I kept seeing the blood seeping under the partition and wondered who she was and whether she was married and had kids and what her family would do without her! And I thought about the young waitress who stopped the man long enough for me to jump onto the seat I was supposed to have been the dead one, was it fate that she had gone to the restrooms just before I did?

As we sped along towards the island, I finally relaxed and put my head back. I fell asleep and didn't wake up until we pulled into the entrance to a Days Inn.

Chapter Fifty

"Hey there sleepyhead, you need to come in with me."

"No way, I'm a total mess. I've been in these same clothes far too long. My hair is a total disaster and I'm beginning to smell really bad. I'm quite capable of sitting locked in this car while you get us checked in."

"I think you should come with me anyway."

"No way. In fact, I'll watch for any and all alien-looking things so you'll be safer coming and going."

"You've got a smart mouth."

"You got that right. Now just go check us in. I'd just draw a lot more attention than we need."

"Good points. You win, but lock the doors and stay alert."

"Yes sir."

I looked around. There was nothing happening in the parking area. Across the lawn someone was mowing the grass, otherwise nothing but the palm trees were moving.

Jim came ambling across to the car. I unlocked the door and he got in and we drove around one side of the motel to park by our room.

A bellhop immediately appeared to help with our luggage. Jim obviously didn't want anyone to see that I had none. He jumped out of the car and sidled up to the old man. He got some money from his wallet and tucked it into the bellhop's hand.

"We're on our honeymoon and would appreciate it if you'd pass the word around that we just want to be left alone. If we need anything we'll call you."

"Very good, sir. Enjoy your stay with us." He winked at Jim and left.

Jim turned to me grinning like a school kid who just got out of school.

"Well, Mrs. Peters, are you ready to begin our honeymoon?"

We went inside our Oceanfront Suite. It had a living room with a queen sofa sleeper, two double beds, and a kitchenette. There was also a micro-fridge unit, a coffee maker, hairdryer and an iron and ironing board. Best of all was the view of the ocean.

"Wow, we could stay here forever."

"Don't get your hopes up."

My feet hadn't had any attention for much too long. I sat down in the closest chair, reached down and took of my slippers and nylons.

"How in hell did you burn your feet. Lying in the sun too long?"

"No, Our Homeland Security Forces are to blame for this."

"Our Homeland Security Forces did that to your feet? What happened?"

I told him everything that happened.

"Jez, Sally. You must have been petrified."

"I was mainly worried that this would ruin our mission."

"You're a gutsy lady!"

"Ayah, I'm glad you know what you're up against."

"I'm beginning to have a suspicion that I've met my match"

"I need to soak my feet in some really cold water and then find a store where I can get some clothes and something to wear besides these slippers."

"You do what you can for your feet and I'll go shopping. Turn the bolt when I leave so nobody can get in."

"And when you get back you'll knock three times so I'll know it's you?"

He stopped, turned toward me and opened his mouth to say something, then changed his mind, grinned at me and left.

I finally was alone. I ran some cold water in the tub, stepped into it and sat down on the edge. Oh, wow, did it ever feel good!

I felt mentally and physically exhausted. I knew that I had to force my mind to go over this whole ordeal. Then maybe I could begin to get on with my life.

I drained out the cold water and let my mind roam at will while I stood quietly under a hot shower. I stayed there until my feet, my body and my mind felt alive again.

I got my last clean underwear out of the backpack and wrapped myself up in a big, fluffy towel. I sat down next to the ocean view window and fell asleep.

Three load knocks on the door startled me awake!

I looked out to make sure it was Jim turned the bolt and opened the door. Jim was standing there holding a new suitcase. He was grinning from ear to ear.

"Hey, pretty lady, can I bunk with you for a few days? I've got a present for you. Can I come in, please?"

Laughing, I moved out of his way and he came inside and locked the door behind him.

He put the suitcase on the rack and opened it up and handed me a bright red sweat suit.

"I don't know why, but I have the feeling that you loved red." Then he gave me a pair of red sandals to match.

"Notice the thick soles to help your hurting feet, and you can even wear them in the water."

Next was a pair of red silk pajamas with slippers to match and then underwear, really brief briefs and a bra. I quickly checked the tags; he had bought the right sizes.

"I just sat there in amazement!

"I found this great women's store, if you don't like these we will go back there just as soon as we have lunch."

"I love them, Jim. Thank you so much!" And then tears started running down my face.

He quickly kneeled down beside me and pulled me close to him. "I didn't mean to make you cry!"

"You didn't. I'm just overwhelmed with your thoughtfulness."

He looked me in the eyes, grinned and wiped away some of my tears.

"Do you think maybe you could get dressed so we could go eat? I'm really awfully hungry – for food too."

I took my wardrobe and went into the bathroom. As I changed into my new clothes, Jim came up to the other side of the door.

"I've been thinking that we need a sort of guideline that we could use if anything goes wrong."

"And you've come up with a plan?"

"Yes, it would probably be good if we acted like newlyweds whenever we go out. You know, like holding hands while we walk, even hug each other – around the waist?"

"That makes sense."

"And I should kiss you – on your cheek – and we should look into each other's eyes and smile a lot."

I was fully dressed by now and I unlocked the door and opened it.

He quickly moved backward and sat down on the end of the bed and put his hands up.

"No, no, please don't hit me."

"You are one crazy bodyguard, where in the world did Sam find you?"

"That's a long story, I'll tell you later but right now I need to finish telling you my plan."

"If I pull you close to me and hug you, it will be because I have a need to check out something going on behind us. Don't panic but if I need to shoot, I'll move you to my left side. I'm right-handed. If this happens you need to quickly drop to the ground and look for something to hide behind. If I get shot, you get away- fast! You ok with all of this?"

"Most of it but if you get shot, I'm not running away. I'll grab your gun and shoot back. My Daddy taught me how to shoot the crows that tried to eat the corn crop every year. I averaged a bird a shot!"

He was quiet for a short while just looking at me. Then he laughed and I laughed with him.

"Damned if you're not a stubborn, tough Maine woman. Let's go eat."

Chapter Fifty-One

We drove along the shore road. The ocean waves were pounding the sandy beaches. You could see miles out across the water to where it seemed to just drop off the world.

"I could ride along this shore forever and never get bored."

"I could too. It's the best way ever to forget your problems and relax."

We turned into the parking lot at the Morgan's Grill. The aroma coming from the outside fan made my stomach know it was hungry.

"I thought we could get quicker service here. I'm really hungry."

"This is great, a hamburger will taste good."

We walked hand in hand to a table where we could watch the sea. We ate quickly and quietly, enjoying the burgers, French fries and soda.

Then we went shopping and put the bags in the car.

"Let's go walking on the beach."

"I'd love to. Are your feet feeling good enough to walk?"

I nodded yes. He locked up the car and we walked hand in hand across the road to the beach.

"That was fun, thanks. I've never shopped with a man before. My late husband and Sam were not really interested in what I bought or wore."

"How long were you married?"

"A long time. I met him when I was a freshman in high school and he was a senior. I was sixteen when we got engaged and we got married the day after I graduated from high school. We had been married quite awhile when he had a fatal heart attack."

"I'm sorry; it must have been tough for you."

"It was, especially knowing that if he had stopped smoking and drinking he could have lived a lot longer. I guess I'm still angry at him for not doing what the doctors told him he had to do to stay alive."

"I know how hard that can be. I haven't had a drink for eighteen years."

"You're an alcoholic?"

"Oh, yes. I lost a big part of my life to alcohol. It's a terrible disease!"

"Well, you've sure done good to stay sober for so long. Many in my family were alcoholics only they wouldn't ever admit they drank. One sister would be so drunk she could hardly stand up and vehemently declare that she didn't drink."

"I probably would still be drinking but I got into some trouble and ended up in jail. I spent a lot of time in the jail library reading all I could about why some people are alcoholics. It helped me understand why I was a drunk."

"You want to tell me why you were in jail?"

"I was driving drunk and hit another car. I probably would still be in jail but one of my friends had some influence and got me moved to a rehab facility. By the time I got out of there I had lost everything I had except my sense of humor and the will to stay sober."

"How did you get connected with this government job?"

"I work for this same friend that helped me get out of jail. He has his own company and we do undercover work and bodyguard word for the government, along with other private jobs.

We had been walking along the shore while we were talking. We found a bench between a couple of dunes and sat quietly for awhile, just watching the waves hit the sand. The dunes blocked off the wind and the sun beat down on us.

"Hey, I'll give you $15,000 if you strip and go in the ocean!"

I looked at him. He was grinning; obviously pleased to think he had shocked me.

"Sure, and I'll give you $20,000 if you can just sit here and watch me and not strip and follow me in!"

He bent over laughing.

"OK, I give up, I can't get the best of you, and I'm going to stop trying to.

"Ayah, I bet you are.

We silently walked back to the car, arms around each other's waists and returned to the motel.

We spent the next few days riding around the South Jekyll Loop. The road weaved its way along the ten miles of public beaches. We stopped at many of them, walking and swimming and sitting between dunes to dry off. He talked a lot more about his life and I talked about mine. We laughed a lot, something I don't do enough of.

Nobody had shown the least bit of interest in me or us. I knew that I soon would need to go back to reality.

"I'm totally rested and I really want and need to go home home.

"Home home? What does home home mean?"

"Oh, once when my 5 year old grandson was visiting from Connecticut, he and I were out walking and he looked up at me and said, "Grammie, I want to go home.""

"We don't have much further to go; we're almost home."

"Grammie, I mean I want to go home home."

"It's been a long since I had a home home and I never thought about it until now. We'll go home home tomorrow."

When nighttime came, we went for a last walk on the beach. A full moon and a sky full of stars looked down on us.

"I always wondered how the stars look like they do, with all of them having five points looking exactly alike."

"They don't have points on them. They are just huge glowing globs of gas that are way out in space, about 23.5 trillion miles out there. What you see as points is just the twinkling caused by movement in our atmosphere. Stars come into our atmosphere as straight lines and the twinkling happens when air movements constantly change the path of the light when it comes through these air movements.

He stopped, sat down on the sand, pulled me down with him and drew a messy circle in the sand.

"That's what stars look like.

We quietly sat in the sand gazing up at the sky.

"Stars can last about 10 billion years. Eventually each star explodes and then it burns out into a dim, cool object. Depending on how large it is, it then becomes a black dwarf, a neutron star, or a black hole."

I think he could have gone on all night. It seemed as if he was in a totally different world. He paused for a minute and I said, "Wow, I think you just burst my star loving bubble. How do you know so much?"

"I have a degree in Science and Mathematics."

"You should be teaching. You've got a real knack for making this interesting."

"This job was sort of a 'do it or else' proposition. It's really a great job and although some people I work with are bastards, I also meet some wonderful people, like you. It helps keep me busy and off the booze."

I held his hand a little tighter.

"I've never talked to anyone about my past before. I hope you don't hate me."

"No way. I admire you for beating the booze and making it to where you are now."

"You're such an easy person to talk to, Hannah. I'll never forget you. Sam is one lucky fellow to have you in his life."

"I'll be your friend forever, Bob. You've taught me so much, from what stars are to how to chill out and laugh. Hopefully we can stay in touch."

We sat together in the sand a long time, not talking just enjoying being together in this time and space.

Bob broke the silence first.

"If we left right now, we can get a flight to Pease Air Force in the morning. Will that work for you?"

"Ayah, let's get on the road again."

He called the Jacksonville Airport and when we arrived an Air Force plane was waiting for us. We both slept all the way to New Hampshire and went to a waiting rental car.

"Oh, show me the way to go home, I'm tired and I want to go to bed."

"I hate to tell you, Bob, but you can't carry a tune in a bucket."

We laughed and I showed him the way to go home.

When we started down the hill to the lake, he stopped. "What a view, so this is your home home."

"Ayah, this is it."

We checked out the garage and the house. Then we walked around the house and down to the lake. Everything was peaceful and quiet. Nothing had changed except me.

"There will be State Policemen staying close by for awhile, some of Sam's old buddies. They'll make sure your safe."

We held hands and walked the cove and back.

We sat down on the dock, dangling our feet over the water.

Bob started rubbing my shoulders and back.

"Are you tense or what, these muscles feel like rocks."

"I almost got killed while Sam and I were in Trinidad."

"Well, no wonder you're tense. Want to tell me about it?"

"I think Sam would be very upset with me if he knew I said anything."

"So, tell me. Nobody else will ever hear what happened."

I can't tell you what we were there for but I can tell you what happened. I told him the story starting with me going into the restroom. He held my hand tighter as I related all the horrid details.

"My God, if that woman hadn't been in the first stall, you'd be dead."

"I know."

I started crying and he hugged me close, still rubbing my shoulders and back.

I calmed down, sat up straight and said, "And that's not all that happened."

"Well, you better tell me the whole story."

I told him about getting involved with a Cuban Government Agency and how I thought for awhile that I might not get out of the room. Then I told him how I was able to get the CD ROM.

"You are something else, Hannah. I'm not sure you should be let out of your cage."

"Well, I'll just write it off as research. It will make good reading in my next book.

"You better hope Sam doesn't ever read that book."

"You got that right."

We sat quietly knowing that this part of our lives was near the end.

"I think I'm going to miss you Bob"

"I know that I'll miss you."

We stood up and silently walked back to the car.

"Well, I better leave now. Oh, why did the chicken cross the road?"

"I don't know why did she cross the road?"

"She heard there was a Chicken Barbeque over there and she was hungry."

"Oh, that's a bad one. Why did she come back across the road?"

"OK, I'll bite, why did she come back across the road?"

"She found out that the barbeque wasn't food for chickens but the chickens were the food."

He growled and said, "You beat me again."

He gave me a quick kiss on my cheek and got into the car.

"Stay safe, Bob. If you ever need to talk, call me."

"Oh, I need to do a whole lot more than talk with you, Hannah. No, no, don't hit me."

He was laughing as he headed up the hill.

I was alone again. I went inside. I made a cup of coffee and went out on the porch. I knew that I should at least start a list of all the things I needed to do but I was having a hard time concentrating on anything. What a strange, awesome, terrifying adventure this had been. I was worried about Sam and wondered where he was now and how long it would be before I heard from him.

Stop worrying, Hannah. You never worried this much before you knew how dangerous his job could be.

Well, I guess I talked myself into relaxing. I stopped pacing back and forth and went back to the kitchen. I fixed a peanut butter and jelly sandwich, made another cup of coffee and went back to the porch. I sat down on the couch, covered up with one of my quilts and listened to the loons calling each other across the lake.

I ate my sandwich, drank my coffee, and went to sleep.

Chapter Fifty-Two

I woke up a little more relaxed than I'd been for quite awhile. I knew that Sarah would be up early so I called her.

"Hi, Mom, glad you're home."

"Me too."

"Did you get some material for your next book?"

"Oh, yes, lots of it."

"Good, I can't wait to read it."

We talked for awhile. She had to leave for work, so we said our goodbyes and hung up.

Then I called Richard. He had already left for breakfast and I left a message saying I was home.

I knew that I should call Abby but I didn't feel ready to get involved with what was happening over there. I needed a little more time to get away from the past two weeks before I tackled any more problems.

I got out my notepad and started writing down all that had happened. I knew that sometime I would use this in one of my murder books; it would make a great story.

I wrote all afternoon, sometimes crying, sometimes shaking like a leaf, but I kept on writing until I had the whole damn story on paper!

A year after I spent twenty-one days in France with a crazy man I was still having nightmares every night. I had taken my own advice back then and I wrote down everything that had happened the year before. I wrote every day for twenty-one days and I got rid of my nightmares! Sarah read what I wrote, and she found someone to publish it. She designed the cover and thought up the title, *Twenty-One Days With A Vulture*!

"That horrid experience became my first book.

With any luck, getting my venture in Cuba written down would not only be a book but would also calm my nerves back down to normal!

Chapter Fifty-Three

The telephone ringing woke me up. Scrambling inside and glanced at the clock. Almost noon! Did I sleep well or what.

The telephone I.D. said that Abby was calling and I answered "Hi Abby, how are you?"

"Oh, Hannah I'm so glad your back. I'm terrible, and so mad. Can you come up here?" She started crying.

"I'll be there just as soon as I can, Abby."

I fumbled around and found something to wear, made a cup of coffee and found my car keys. The CRV started on the first try and I backed out of the garage, shut the door and locked it. When I did get back I wanted to know that my home was secure!

On the way to the Federal Housing I wondered what had happened now. What else

267

could possibly go wrong? I turned off the highway, started up the mountain road and the problem was staring me in the face!

There were no trees left behind the buildings and most of the boulders were gone. The eagle's nest was no longer there.

Abby was in the parking lot waiting for me. I parked, got out and we hugged, then turned and looked up the mountain.

I stared in disbelief. There was a huge tower where the eagles had lived for years and the entire area was surrounded by a 6 ft. metal fence.

"They can't do this. Bald eagles are an endangered species and their nesting areas are protected.

Abby sobbed. "One of the Cleeve crews came in early one morning, cut all the trees and bulldozed the boulders off the side of the mountain. Within a few hours another crew was here putting up the tower and a day later the fence was finished and everyone had left."

As we stood there we heard a faint cackling sound – kik - ik – ik - ik, kleek – kleek – kleek We looked up. High up in the sky, the two bald eagles were soaring in circles over what had been their domain!

Abby stopped crying and angrily said, "I watched them each day, and I yelled at them. I called the Town Office. I called the State and nobody did anything to stop them. They didn't give a damn that Bald Eagles are an endangered species and that it was against the law to destroy their nesting areas. Nobody cared at all! You can just bet that there's been a whole lot of money put into a whole lot of pockets to get this atrocity accomplished!"

She was shaking all over and started sobbing again.

"It's getting cold out here Abby. Let's go inside and make hot tea and try to figure out what we can do next about this."

We went inside, I made some tea and Abby began to calm down.

"This is punishment for us telling on them about all the things they did wrong on this place. They are already back here 'fixing' some of the problems."

"The first thing they did was to take out this inner door so there wouldn't be a small entrance into the living room any more."

"I didn't even notice that when we came in. Well, that's an improvement."

She wheeled over to the picture window.

"We all have air conditioners now. Look what they did."

I went over to look and Abby pushed a wooden panel to one side and stuck her arm out the window.

"They cut the hole in the glass too big for the small air conditioners they put in so the added a sliding piece of wood. With no inner door there anymore you can move this sliding piece of wood and reach in to unlock your door. Anybody can get into your house anytime they want to."

We both sat there in stunned silence!

"That bastard realtor up on the mountain top would sell his soul for the almighty dollar, and that Code Enforcement Officer would sell her soul for a good fuck! What a rotten combination they are! Oh, damn, what will the eagles do?"

We sat quietly for a minute.

"I'm pretty sure the eagles will hang around here. They probably have a second nest farther up the mountain, or they wouldn't still be here. But that still doesn't make it right."

"If I could have gotten my hands on their necks, I think I would have strangled them."

"I agree with you that those two excuses for humans have probably paid off everyone involved so nothing will ever be done."

"Yeah, and they're up there now, having a huge party, probably celebrating with all the money they all made on the cell phone tower. The cars have been roaring up past here all afternoon. Speed limits don't mean anything to them."

"Let's get some jackets on and wander around outside. At least we can watch the eagles flying!"

We walked around the complex. Abby showed me some improvements that had already been made.

"They have started putting on bigger outside doors with storm and screen doors. They have rebuilt these wooden stairs. I watched as they dug post holes and poured cement to hold the uprights from wobbling."

"Dumpster Dam and the Trash Man are working together just great. What a relief to never have to smell road-kill cooking anymore. That was a great idea, Hannah."

We went back to her unit, made more tea and went back outside to sit and watch the eagles.

Chapter Fifty-Four

Up on the mountain the party was in full swing. Loud music blared out over the lake. Food was served and the liquor bar was open for all. A big sign over the bar said, 'HELP YOURSELF.' Everyone was doing as they were told.

Clarence was drunk before the party even started and by the time everyone else was plastered, he was close to passing out. He wandered outside, began throwing up and toppled into the moat! He surfaced once and yelled for help but nobody heard him. He went under again and stayed there. Nobody missed him so nobody went looking for him.

Inside, Clayton was chasing Molly around. He finally caught up to her.

"Drinking makes me horny as all hell! Come on, you're going for a ride with me and do one of your great jobs on me!"

He dragged her out to the car, and she had his fly unzipped before he got in. She was on the front seat floor by the time he slid behind the wheel.

"Way to go, Molly. You are good!"

They headed down the mountain road, oblivious to how fast they were going or how poorly he was driving.

Abby and I heard the car racing down the hill and turned from watching the eagles to watch for the car to appear.

As it approached it was obvious that it was out of control, it was weaving back and forth across the road and going way too fast!

As it sped past us, it looked like Clayton was alone. Just before he would have to brake for the sharp curve, we heard the sound of the eagle. She swooped down across the hood of the car, and then rose high in the air with another loud kik – ik – ik – id, kleek – kleek – kleek!

Clayton never even had a chance to hit his brakes, even if he had been sober!

The car careened straight ahead, took of into the air and then flew down the mountain. Moments later we heard it crash, probably into the boulders that he had just had pushed down there.

"I'll go in and call 911."

"Good, I'll work my way down to the car. I doubt if he could have lived through this but if he did, the quicker someone can help him the better."

Abby headed for the phone.

"Abby, don't mention the bald eagle, OK?"

"What bald eagle?"

I ran into the woods and started down the hill to the crashed car.

Chapter Fifty-Five

I carefully worked my way down through trees, bushes and boulders. What a mess! It was slippery going on the pine needles that covered the ground and it was extremely steep.

Two of three times I started to slide, grabbed onto a branch and then kept going. It seemed like it took me forever to get there. I was trying to hurry but I knew that I couldn't help anyone if I fell!

When I got down to the crash site, the car was jammed between a huge pine tree and a large boulder. It was still swaying a little as it hung about two feet off the ground. I cautiously moved closer. The driver's side door was hanging open, almost torn from the car. I looked around and saw Clayton a few feet away, hanging lifeless from a branch of a large pine tree. He was almost totally decapitated and his legs hung loosely from what was left of his body. His fly was unzipped and blood was pouring from what was left of his genitalia!

I turned away but not soon enough. I felt faint and my stomach erupted! I sank onto the ground, closed my eyes tightly hoping that the horror I had just seen would vanish from my brain.

I slowly regained some composure and realized that I needed to check the car. Maybe there had been someone with Clayton.

I worked my way carefully back to the wreckage. It was still swaying a little and I got as near as I dared to and looked in the open door.

Molly was squeezed under the dash board and between the seats and the dashboard. The front of the car had been crumpled and pushed almost into the windshield. She looked as if she was only 8 inches wide. She was totally crushed and hardly recognizable!

I staggered away from this horrible scene of death. I found another rock and sat down again, taking huge gulps of air, trying to calm my racing heart!

277

The car was still slowly swaying back and forth, going slower all the time. The broken tree branches had stopped falling and found a place to lay until they would rot into the ground years from now. The car finally stopped its groaning and was still!

I put my head down into my hands and sat there with tears streaming down my face. What a horrible way to die! Nobody deserved to be killed like this. I mentally revisited all the accidents that I had gone to as an EMT. None of them even began to be as ghastly as this one.

I sat there and tried to stop crying. I had come so close to being killed a few days before! How come some people are spared and others aren't? Is there really a God who controls whose turn is next?

I hadn't prayed for a long time but I did now. I sat there and prayed for the souls of these two mutilated people.

I gradually became aware that there was no noise. It was a sinister silence unlike anything I had ever experienced before. As I sat there in awe, a strange, unearthly noise pierced the stillness!

My whole body shook! I told myself that it probably was just a gust of wind blowing through the wreckage, but I would have sworn that I had just heard the bald eagle laughing.

Historical Note:

A Cleeve did sail from Bristol, England aboard the Swift in April l630! His name was George Cleeve and he was the founder of Portland, Maine. He did not, however, sire four sons; he had one child, a girl. All the rest of the information in this book regarding the Cleeves is also fiction.

There is, however, an interesting true story regarding the real Mr. Cleeve.

Mr. Cleeve and another gentleman, Mr. Winter were both granted the same territory in Maine by the King of England. Mr. Winter lived on Richmond Island in Casco Bay and had one descendant, a daughter. The Rev. Robert Jordan married this daughter. When Mr. Winter died, Rev. Jordan inherited all the Winter property.

Mr. Cleeve and Rev. Jordan fought over this territory and when the first court convened in Portland in the 1600s, they took each other to court. A judge divided this territory between the two men. Mr. Cleeve got Portland and part of South Portland.

Rev. Jordan got part of South Portland, all of Cape Elizabeth and Richmond Island. The

Jordan ancestors still own land in this section of Maine.

Neither Mr.Cleeve nor the Rev. Jordan were happy with this decision and remained antagonists to the end.

I am a descendant of George Cleeve and in l950 I married a descendant of the Rev. Jordan. At that time we did not know that we had ended a 300-year-old feud. I believe that our son and daughter are the only descendants of both these founders of the Casco Bay region in Maine.*

*Some of the historical information re: George Cleeve was researched by Alice Mitchell Branson. This information appeared in the *"George Cleeve Family Registry"*

Printed for the Greater Portland 350th Celebration. The Cleeve ancestors gathered at the Cleeve Monument, on the Eastern Promenade in Portland overlooking Casco Bay. I was there for this memorable event.

EVORA JORDAN

Books by Evora Jordan

Twenty-One Days with a Vulture
ISBN: 0-9725071-1-6

Twenty One days in France with a trusted colleague and a gentleman turned into a frightening journey with a vulgar, irrational, paranoid, obsessive con man. Hannah used all her abuse counselor and survival skills to get home alive.

Annie Love
ISBN: 0-9725071-2-4

A Children's Book "Annie Love" is Annie's story - a true story of her journey from abuse and sadness to survival and hope, recovery and happiness.

Hannah Gray Cook Book
ISBN: 0-9725071-3-2

Great cooking starts with a little bit of reading. Enjoy some tidbits about Hannah gray Murder Mystery Books while cooking up your own kitchen mystery.

Tainted Sand
ISBN: 0-9725071-0-8

An awesome work of fiction inspired by a true murder mystery. A man says his wife disappeared in a small store in Maine. Evidence indicates that she was killed in their home in Massachusetts. Her body was never found. He has not been charged for her murder.

Purchase a signed copy directly from the Publisher

Company (optional) : _____
Name: _____
Address: _____
City: _____ State: _____ Zip: _____

Book	Price	Quantity
Tainted Towers ISBN: 0-9725071-4-0	$11.95	_____
Tainted Sand ISBN: 0-9725071-0-8	$7.95	_____
Annie Love ISBN: 0-9725071-2-4	$7.95	_____
Twenty-One Days with a Vulture ISBN: 0-9725071-1-6	$7.95	_____
Hannah Gray's Cook Book ISBN: 0-9725071-3-2	$14.95	_____
Total	$_____	_____

Please add $2 for the first book and $1 for each additional book for shipping and handling within the United States. $5 for International orders.   Send your order to:

Evora Books LLC
P.O. Box 397
Canton, CT 06019

Or visit the website at www.BooksByEvora.com